"I cannot take much more of this. Let us go to your bedchamber. I want you, now!"

Moira drew back and blinked dumbly. "Mr. Hartly!" she said. "I hope you do not think I am that sort of girl!"

A bark of laughter erupted in the still air. "I know exactly what sort of girl you are, milady. Come, why waste time? Or is there a fee to be settled first? Is that it?"

"What—what do you mean?" she asked in perplexity.

"I mean, do you charge for your services, or is this an exercise in mutual gratification?"

A mask of outrage seized her features. "Mr. Hartly! You had better leave at once."

Also by Joan Smith
Published by Fawcett Books:

OLD LOVER'S GHOST
NO PLACE FOR A LADY
THE GREAT CHRISTMAS BALL
AUTUMN LOVES: An Anthology
THE SAVAGE LORD GRIFFIN
GATHER YE ROSEBUDS

REGENCY MASQUERADE

Joan Smith

FAWCETT CREST • NEW YORK

A Fawcett Crest Book
Published by Ballantine Books

Library of Congress Catalog Card Number: 94-94198

ISBN 0-449-22276-4

Manufactured in the United States of America

First Edition: August 1994

10 9 8 7 6 5 4 3 2 1

Chapter One

"I must say, it don't look the sort of place a well-greased villain like Lionel March would run to ground," Jonathon Trevithick said doubtfully. "With all the blunt he stole from us, you would think he could afford to put up at the Pulteney, in London."

The two occupants of the carriage peered out the window at a quaint inn, whose bottom story was composed of flint and stone, its upper story of brick and timber, topped with a thatched roof. There were many such old buildings in this chalky corner of Kent, where native building materials were scarce and the builders had to improvise. Despite its mongrel facade, the inn had the charm of antiquity. Red roses clambered up either side of the doorway. The windows were entirely concealed by a growth of yews. The sign suspended over the doorway showed a crude painting of an owl, with the words OWL HOUSE INN painted in black on a gilt background.

"He must be hiding out. Unless he has turned

smuggler, there is very little hereabouts to appeal to one of his habits," Miss Trevithick replied, in accents that indicated Mr. March's habits were deep-dyed in worldliness.

Blaxstead, the village on the southeast coast of England where the carriage had stopped, was ideally situated for smuggling and little else, except perhaps fishing. It was a mile from the coast, but an estuary ran into the village. At high tide, a few fishing boats and one seagoing barge were to be seen. The Owl House Inn sat on a point of land overlooking the estuary, and beyond it, to the flat marshlands reclaimed from the sea. The sky was pearly gray, with a lowering sun tinting one patch of cloud to copper.

"What a wretched place," Jonathon said. "I hope it don't take us long to steal back our money."

"You should not use the word 'steal,' Jonathon," Moira said severely. "We are here to recoup what is rightfully ours. And once we leave this carriage, we have used our own names for the last time. There must be no slipups. I doubt Mr. March will recognize us, but you may be sure he remembers our names."

She cast a worried look at Jonathon. He was hardly old enough to act as her protector. A young lady her age really ought to have a chaperon. As she was posing as a widow, however, it was not strictly necessary. If anyone questioned it, she would behave in a haughty manner that left no doubt of her ability to chaperon herself.

Moira felt they were bound to create a commotion at the inn when they registered as Sir David and Lady Crieff. The titles suggested they were man and wife, yet Jonathon was obviously too young for the role. It would soon be known he was her stepson. Sir Aubrey Crieff had married a lady young enough to be his daughter. He had a son, David, by his first wife. Upon Sir Aubrey's death, David had assumed the "sir."

Jonathon read her concern. "I do not like to think of a green girl like you posing as a dashing widow, Moira," he said. "There might be some ugly customers putting up at a place like this. Smugglers are known as 'owlers' in these parts, because they work at night, I daresay. To judge by its name and location, this could be a smuggling inn."

"We shan't bother the Gentlemen, and they shan't bother us. This is our only chance to recover our money," Moira said, her chin squaring in determination. "All I have to do is look haughty and wear the fine gowns we begged and borrowed. March is more likely to make up to a rich widow than to a provincial damsel."

Jonathon had little doubt March would be chasing after her, even without the added bait of a valuable jewelry collection. At least three of the fellows at home were tagging at her skirts, and that without a sou of dowry. Moira was certainly a beauty. She took after Papa's side of the family, so March would not recognize a family resemblance. He had never met Mr. Trevithick. Moira's raven black hair and ivory complexion turned heads wherever she went. But it was her lustrous silver-gray eyes with lashes a yard long that were her real claim to beauty.

March had caught only a glimpse of Moira when she returned from her ladies' seminary in Farnham for the funeral. He would not recognize that bawling schoolgirl with red eyes as Lady Crieff. He would hear the word "heiress" and see nothing but another fortune to be stolen.

Jonathon thought it was a wonder the way Moira had taken hold of the reins when her mama died, leaving her burdened with that wretched mortgage, and all their money gone. Mrs. Trevithick's sister had stayed with them for three years, but it was not the aunt who had run the ship. It was Moira, and she a mere chit of fifteen years at the time. Yes, if anyone could carry off this desperate charade, it was Moira.

Lionel March had never seen Jonathon at all, as he was away at school during the courtship and quarantined with chicken pox for the funeral. Jonathon had got his looks from the other side of the family. Like his mama, he had blue eyes and light blond hair. At sixteen years, he had attained a height of six feet but had not yet fleshed out either his frame or his face. He was at that awkward age when it was impossible for his jackets and trousers to keep pace with his ever-growing limbs. His particular bane was his nose, which had mushroomed overnight from a button to a fair-sized wedge, effectively removing any telltale likeness to his mama.

"Are you sure you will recognize him after all this time?" Jonathon asked.

"I would recognize his hide in a tanning factory," Moira said, her voice hardening to bitterness.

"There is always his finger, in any case," Jonathon added. "That bit missing off the small finger of his left hand."

Moira knew she would need no such clue. Lionel March's face was engraved in her memory. It had haunted her in a hundred nightmares. He had come like a spoiler into the simple lives of the Trevithicks, wreaking havoc. How could Mama have cared for him? He was the devil incarnate. Yet within the space of six weeks he had talked her mama into marriage, and Papa scarcely dead a year. If only she had been home . . . But Mama had been alone, and lonesome. No one in the neighborhood knew a thing about March. He had claimed to be a large landowner from Cornwall. His fancy wardrobe and carriage suggested money. Their relatives had warned Mrs. Trevithick to caution, but she had paid them no heed. She had rushed pell-mell into marriage with a man she scarcely knew, and within three months she lay dead in her grave.

It would not have surprised Moira if the villain had killed her, but it seemed March was at least not guilty of that. He had been in London on business when Mama took that tumble from her mount. It was only after the funeral that the Trevithicks learned the extent of his depredations on the estate. Papa had left the Elms unencumbered, with a dowry of ten thousand for Moira besides. The dowry was gone, and the estate had been mortgaged for fifteen thousand pounds. After the funeral, Mr. March had told the solicitor he was running up to London for a few days to arrange finances with his man of business.

He never returned. He had stolen twenty-five thousand pounds, and Moira had made a vow that she would recover it, if she had to follow March to Africa or the North Pole to do it. Their solicitor had told them the theft had been done legally. As their mama's husband, March had the right to manage—or mismanage—her monies as he saw fit. If the law could not help them, then they must help themselves.

It was only after his departure that the rumors began surfacing. It seemed Mr. March had bilked a certain young lord out of a fortune at cards six months before coming to the Elms, the Trevithick's family estate in Surrey. Before that, he had been promoting shares in a nonexistent gold mine in Canada. He had married a wealthy, aging widow in Devon and made off with her fortune—unfortunately after marrying Mrs. Trevithick, making both marriages legal. There was some possibility he might have other wives sequestered about the country as well, but if so, they had not come to light.

It was discovered he had used various aliases and disguises in his career. He had been a black-haired sea captain with whiskers, a blond, clean-shaven gentleman farmer from America, an Irish horse breeder, and, on one occasion, a bishop. But the villain in each case had one physical characteristic he could not change: He was missing the tip of the small finger on his left hand.

It had taken four years of inquiry, letter writing, and scanning the journals for reports of his victims, and at last it had paid off. The determination to catch him had been all that had kept her going through the lean years of scrimping and trying to keep the Elms afloat. Lady Marchbank of Blaxstead, a second cousin of Mr. Trevithick, had seen a stranger missing the appropriate bit of finger in a shop in her village. She had followed him and learned he was staying at Owl House Inn, using the name Major Stanby. As this was such an out-of-the-way spot, she assumed he was in hiding from his latest victim. She had kindly invited the

Trevithicks to put up with her at Cove House, but Moira, who was in charge of the expedition, had elected to stay at the inn, as that would give her greater access to March.

Over the past four years, the strategy for recovering their money had changed with the times. It was only last year that Moira had read the story of Lady Crieff, from Scotland. It seemed an aging baronet had married his shepherd's daughter, a female decades younger than himself. Upon his demise, the female had inherited an awesome collection of jewelry valued at one hundred thousand pounds. The reason the story had received such widespread attention had to do with the son, David, now Sir David Crieff. His lawyers had undertaken litigation to recover the jewels. As they were of more value than the family estate, the lawyers were claiming Sir Aubrey had been deranged when he had made the will. Naturally he would wish his son to be his major heir.

After scouring the journals for a month, Moira had discovered a short piece stating that the lawyers were endeavoring to settle the case of Crieff vs. Crieff out of court. The article did not say who would likely end up with the jewels; thus it was eligible to pretend that Lady Crieff had them and was on her way to London to sell them. Sir David, a mere stripling, would be under her sway. Of course, the sale would be illegal at this time, but Moira doubted Mr. March would be much concerned as to the rightful owner.

A few details had been given about the collection. There was a fabulous set of emerald necklace and ear pendants, a sapphire necklace, various diamonds, and a ruby ring. With this scanty description to guide her, Moira had purchased paste pieces similar to the Crieff jewels. Her own diamond necklace was to be the bait in the trap set for Stanby. In some manner, she meant to inveigle him into buying the collection of ersatz jewels with real money. Her diamond necklace was genuine, an heirloom left to her by her paternal aunt. Fortunately it had not been with her mama's jewels, and thus it had escaped Mr. March's grasping fingers.

Moira knew the scheme was fraught with peril, but what worried her most was Jonathon's ability to carry off the charade. He was clever enough and certainly eager, but so young. She was careful not to allow her doubts to show, but when she was alone in bed at night, she admitted reluctantly that perhaps she, at nineteen years, was no match for that hardened criminal, Lionel March. She might inadvertently make a slip. Of greater concern, March might abduct her to gain his ends. She would have to be constantly on her guard.

When she began gathering up her reticule and padlocked jewelry case, Jonathon said, "Are you ready, Lady Crieff?"

"Yes, let us go, Sir David. There, you see, we have both remembered our new names. Come along, David. I think I should call you David, without using your title. What do you think?"

"It sounds more natural, though I should like to be a sir. Should I call you Mama?"

Moira considered it a moment. "Would a young man call such a youthful stepmother Mama? I rather think Sir Aubrey would have encouraged it. But no, Lady Crieff would rule the roost, and she, I think, would prefer her title."

"As she was only a shepherd's daughter, you ought not to act too much like a lady, eh?"

"A young woman who would marry a much older man for his money would put on great airs once she had achieved her aim of becoming a lady. Mind you, Lady Crieff may slip into vulgarity from time to time, and drop a few aitches." She tapped the window to summon the groom to let down the stairs.

"Do I look all right, David?" she asked.

His blue eyes traveled from her feathered bonnet to her dark green sarcenet mantle and gloved hands. He was happy to see Moira dressed up as she ought to be.

"Like a duchess, madam," he replied.

The groom, a faithful family retainer who was aware of the charade, opened the door and let down the steps for the Crieffs to alight. Moira handed him a padlocked jewelry case. The passengers looked all around, hoping for a sight of Mr. March. He was not to be seen, but a new object of interest arrived at that instant. A dashing yellow curricle drawn by a pair of matched grays drove up smartly beside them. A groom from the inn came running forth. The man tossed him the reins and descended from his perch. He looked at the Trevithicks' carriage with considerable interest. That interest, of course, was centered on the incomparable Moira. When he stopped in his tracks and stared at her in admiration, Jonathon felt a twinge of apprehension.

Moira noticed the gentleman, too, and thought he was something out of the ordinary. She allowed herself a swift examination. His face had the weathered complexion of the sportsman, and his eyes were the flashing eyes of mischief. He was outfitted in the highest kick of fashion, from the curled beaver tilted rakishly over one eye to the toe of his shining Hessians. A jacket of blue Bath cloth clung to his broad shoulders, displaying an intricate cravat and a waistcoat striped in yellow and mulberry. A malacca cane and York tan gloves completed his ensemble. She had not expected to encounter so much elegance at a small village inn.

He lifted his hat as Moira passed. A cap of black hair was briefly visible before the curled beaver resumed its place. Moira's instinct was to snub this fast behavior. She caught herself just in time. She was no longer Moira Trevithick; she was that dashing creature, Lady Crieff. She cast a flirtatious smile over her shoulder as David held the inn door for her to enter.

The gentleman honored her with an answering smile and a bow. It was no ordinary smile. Moira read its message as clearly as if he had spoken it. He admired her; he was eager for her acquaintance—and he seemed the sort of gentleman who would go after what he wanted buckle and thong.

"Watch your step," Jonathon said.

Moira stole another peek at the gentleman. He was still staring at her. The predatory gleam in his eye sent shivers up her spine.

When they were inside, Jonathon said, "By the living jingo, did you see that team of grays? Blood prads! I wager they were doing sixteen miles an hour. Wouldn't I love to get my hands on the ribbons."

Before Moira could reply, the inn door opened and the same gentleman entered. He followed them to the desk. While Moira entered their names in the registry, the man spoke to the clerk.

"Do you have a Major Stanby staying with you?" he asked, in a deep, masculine voice.

"Why, yes, sir," the innkeeper replied. "He has taken the northeast suite at the back of the inn. He has stepped out, however. We are expecting him back for dinner."

The name Major Standby caused Moira and Jonathon to exchange a meaningful glance. She shook her head slightly to let Jonathon know he was not to speak. Her fingers trembled, but in the twinkling of a bedpost she had recovered and continued registering while the man talked to the clerk. David took the jewelry case from the groom and led Moira upstairs.

They had hired two bedrooms, with a sitting room between for their mutual use. It was the best suite the inn had to offer, but it was by no means elegant. The ceiling slanted sharply at the edges of the rooms. The chambers were clean and bright, however, with a view of the estuary from the windows. The uneven plank floors were partly covered with a braided rug. Moira's bed had a simple cambric canopy and an oval mirror above the toilet table.

"It ain't exactly like home," Jonathon said doubtfully.

"It looks comfortable enough, though I daresay Lady Crieff will find a few items to complain about." This settled, she discussed more interesting matters. "It seems Major Stanby has picked up an accomplice since he bilked us out of our fortune. I knew from the way that fellow was grinning at me that he was up to no good."

"Very likely you are right," Jonathon agreed, "although to be fair, you grinned at him first. We do not know he is working with Mr. March, just because he was inquiring for him."

"That is true. March has always worked alone in the past."

"P'raps the word is out that March is setting up a game of cards. You know cheating at cards is another of his tricks. We ought to warn Mr. Hartly."

"Is that his name?" Moira asked. "Sharp of you to have noticed, Jon—David."

"That is the name he gave the innkeeper. I should love to have a ride in that curricle."

"No need to rush things. We shall keep an eye on Hartly. He might prove useful. One never knows how things will turn out."

"I hope they turn out so that I get behind that team."

"I wonder if they have assemblies at this inn," Moira said, with a pensive look. "Don't look at me like that, David. I have no intention of throwing my bonnet at Mr. Hartly, but it would be an unexceptionable way to meet March and also become a little acquainted with Mr. Hartly, to discover what he is doing here, asking for Stanby."

She said no more, but it occurred to her that if he was not Stanby's colleague, he might be willing to become hers. She would feel a deal safer with a strong, older masculine ally.

"Do you mean to set up a flirtation with Hartly?"

"No, that would be too obvious." Then she added with a sly smile, "But I might let him set up one with me, if he has a mind to."

"That sounds vulgar enough for Lady Crieff, taking up with a stranger. Pity I am not the one who must be vulgar. I could do it better than you."

"We shall see about that! I can tie my garter in

public as well as the next hussy. Now, where should we hide the jewels?"

"You could ask the innkeeper to put them in his safe. Or shall I do it?"

"You do it, and make a show of concern for their safety. Wait until he is alone, and tell him the case is very valuable."

"So it is—to us. We hope to exchange this collection of glass for our fortune."

He picked up the padlocked case and went whistling downstairs.

Chapter Two

Before Mr. Hartly left the desk, he said to the innkeeper, "About Major Stanby . . . I do not actually have his acquaintance. I pray you do not tell him I was inquiring for him. It is to be a surprise." As he spoke, he slid a gold coin onto the counter, from whence it found its way into the innkeeper's pocket with the swiftness of a frog snapping up a fly.

Jeremy Bullion tapped his finger to his nose, nodded his head, and gave a wink of his sharp, snuff-colored eye. "Any little thing I can do for you, sir, ye have only to ask and Jeremy Bullion will be happy to oblige. Folks call me Bullion."

"Very good. You are raw metal, but pure gold, I have no doubt."

Bullion accepted this fatigued compliment with a smile. "Aye, sir. I may be lump gold, but I am twenty-four karat. If ye'd care for a sandwich in your room, or a bottle of wine, ye've only to give the bell chord a yank. As to your duds, the wife's as good as a seamstress for mending up a tear or pressing a jacket."

"How very kind, but my valet will be joining me soon. Did Stanby give any idea how long he plans to stay?"

"He's hired his suite by the week, hasn't he?"

Mr. Hartly's face eased into a smile. "That will be all for now, Bullion. Ah, one other thing. I shall require a private dining parlor for this evening."

Bullion's craggy face wrinkled into a very mask of sorrow. "Now, there I must disoblige you, sir. We're but a small establishment. I've one public room for commoners—farmers and such—and a Great Room for the Quality, like yourself. I could have dinner took up to your bedchamber—no trouble at all. Or I could put you in the corner of the Great Room, with a folding screen around the table. You'd never know you wasn't alone in the world."

With a memory of the delightful young lady he had seen descending from her carriage, Hartly said, "No need to hide me in a corner, Bullion. I shall keep my face to the wall to prevent turning anyone's stomach." This was greeted with a bark of laughter from Bullion. "If you'd care to seat me next to Lady Crieff's party, I should be obliged. The lady is not from these parts, I daresay?"

"Scotland," Bullion replied, pointing to the register. He looked about to see that no spies were listening, lifted his fingers to hide his lips, and said in a confidential manner, "But she's connected to these parts. Lady Marchbank arranged her rooms. Old Lord Marchbank's lady. He owns half the county. Sends his man up to Parliament and all. A powerful gent, the old gaffer."

"I wonder why Lady Crieff is not putting up with the Marchbanks."

"That wouldn't be for me to say, but I fancy there's a reason." He gave a wise nod, which conveyed nothing to Hartly.

A red-faced woman in a large white apron appeared around the corner. "The fire's going out, Bullion, and Wilf is busy in the stable."

Bullion gave a sheepish smile to his guest. "The good wife," he said, and darted off.

Mr. Hartly went abovestairs, pondering why Lady Crieff was not welcome at the home of her noble friends, the Marchbanks.

It was soon clear to Jeremy Bullion that he had not one swell but two under his roof. Not long after Mr. Hartly went abovestairs, his traveling carriage and team of four arrived. A slender, know-it-all young dandy with a womanly face came prancing in demanding a suite of rooms for his master, Mr. Hartly. He went into a fit of hysterics upon learning that his master had reached the inn before him.

"And I not here to air the chambers and arrange his bath! Damme, I ought to be horsewhipped. What will he do without me?"

"Ye'd be his valet, I'm thinking," Bullion said, unmoved by the fellow's ranting.

Mott bowed. "I have the honor, sir, to be Mr. Hartly's valet and traveling factotum, Mott."

"Bullion," Bullion said, offering his hand.

Mott reluctantly touched the tip of his fingers, then quickly withdrew his hand. "Has my master been here long?"

"Not above ten minutes."

Mott breathed a sigh of relief. "Then he has not endeavored a fresh toilette without me. We shall require a tub of hot water. No need for towels. We travel with our own linens. Have your servants bring up the case of claret in the carriage. It must be carried gently so as not to disturb the dregs. We dine at seven. I shall be in the kitchen to oversee the preparations of my master's dinner."

Bullion found himself on the horns of a nasty dilemma. It went against the pluck to disoblige a wealthy guest; on the other hand, Maggie would brook no interference in her kitchen.

"You can speak to Cook about that," he said, washing his hands of the matter.

"Just so. Now let me see your private dining parlors, my good Bullion."

"Mr. Hartly's already arranged that."

Mott adopted a pout. "I trust it does not have a western exposure. My master likes the drapes open. I would not want the setting sun in his eyes."

"That'll be no problem at all," Bullion said, with a thought to the dim cavern where his worthy customers dined. No ray of sun had penetrated those panes for a century. The yew hedge growing outside them was better than a curtain.

"Good. Now I must go to my master, if you will direct me thither."

"The yellow suite, left at the top o' the stairs."

"You won't forget the hot water," Mott said, and went off, staggering under the weight of a large wicker basket, presumably holding his master's towels and bed linen.

Bullion shook his head at the freakish ways of the ton. Hartly would call the shots, however, and he seemed a deal easier to please than the mincing valet.

As soon as Mott left Bullion, his prissy expression faded. When he tapped at the door of the yellow suite and went in, there was no mincing gait or fluting voice.

He plopped the wicker basket on the floor, grinned, and said, "Well, here we are. Have you seen Stanby yet?"

"No, but he's putting up here for a week," Hartly replied. "What kept you, Rudolph?"

"Lost a wheel just outside of London."

"Playing hunt the squirrel, I warrant."

"Willoughby put me to the dare. I ran him clean off the road. I put on a good act for old Bullion. He's sending up bathwater."

"Damn the bathwater. Where is the wine?"

"It's coming—ah, here it is."

When he opened the door, he was wearing his inane smile and gave a good imitation of a fool. "Mind you don't jiggle it, lads. That is rare good stuff you're handling. Shall I draw a cork, master?" he asked, turning to Hartly.

"If you would be so kind, Mott. Give the lads a pourboire, there's a good fellow."

Mott reached into his pocket and handed the two servants a generous pourboire. Then he turned to the dresser and scowled at the wineglasses on a tray.

"They call these tumblers wineglasses!" he exclaimed, with a shake of his head. "We would not use them in our kitchen."

As soon as the servants left, he drew a cork and filled the glasses. Handing one to Hartly, he lifted his glass and said, "To success. I shall follow your orders in peace as I did in war, Major. Dashed kind of you to help me."

"I am happy for the chance. I find England just a

tad dull after the recent excitements of the Peninsula. And by the by, cuz, I am Mr. Hartly here. Let us not confuse our personas."

"Damn, I don't have to act the foolish valet when we are alone, I hope?"

"You do not have to act quite so convincingly even when we are not alone. I suspect you harbor a love of the stage and are enjoying the role."

"I enjoy the prospect of meeting Major Stanby, the bounder. I would give a monkey to know where he is and what he is doing."

"I hope to meet him this evening. It seems we members of the ton will be dining en masse. Bullion has no private dining parlors."

"He did not say so when I asked. Said you'd already arranged that."

"So I have. He suggested hiding me in a corner behind a screen. I opted for a table next to Lady Crieff, a pretty lady putting up here. The name sounds familiar." He looked a question at Mott.

"So it does," Mott replied, refilling his glass, "though I cannot say I have met her. What does she look like?"

"Like a black-haired angel, with a devilish eye in her head. Young. The fellow traveling with her is called Sir David Crieff. I noticed a 'Bart.' after his name in the registry. A baronet. He is not old enough to be her husband, yet he is too old to be a son. He cannot be her brother, or she would not be Lady Crieff. That title is reserved for his wife. An odd business, is it not?"

"Demmed odd. You don't figure she could be a lightskirt who ain't quite clear how titles work? I mean to say, just calling herself Lady Crieff?"

"That leaps to mind, of course. The lady has a

roguish smile. On the other hand, Bullion tells me she is a friend of Lady Marchbank, a local worthy. I doubt she has anything to do with Stanby, in any case."

"Unless he has taken up with a bit o' muslin," Mott added. "If she is as pretty as you say, she would attract victims for him."

"She'll want watching. I noticed her servant was carrying a padlocked case—jewelry, presumably. Selling paste for diamonds might be a new rig Stanby is running."

"Have you any notion how to approach Stanby?"

"When he sees my curricle and traveling carriage, and my excellent valet, I venture to say he will accost me."

"Yes, and then what?"

"I shall let him make the first move. A game of cards is one possibility."

"Mind you don't drink from his bottle, or let him use his own deck."

"I shall drink only tap ale—or my own excellent claret," Hartly replied, lifting his glass in a toast.

"Will he have as much as fifteen thousand with him, I wonder? That is the sum we are going for."

"If he does not have it with him, he can get it. He is high in the stirrups. It stands to reason."

"I despise the fellow. Hanging is too good for him."

"I trust it will not come to murder," Hartly said blandly. "We have shed enough blood. After all, Rudolph, we are officers and gentlemen."

"And that is another thing," Mott said, beginning to rant now. "Posing as an officer. He gives the military a bad name. I doubt he ever wore a uniform. Ask him where he served, when you meet him."

"No, no. We do not want him to suspect we harbor such a pernicious thing as a brain in our heads. We shall rob him most politely, like the gentlemen we are, cousin."

They were interrupted by a tap at the door. Mott admitted two serving girls carrying in a tub of hot water.

Mott fussed about, dipping in his finger and scolding that the water was too hot. "Fetch up a pitcher of cold water. No, never mind. We shall let the water cool and my master will have his bath later. You may tell Cook I shall be down shortly to discuss my master's dinner with her."

The girls exchanged a wide-eyed grin and bounced out.

"I shall dart down to the kitchen now and begin making up to those chits while you have your bath," Mott said. "Servants always know what is going on at an inn. We might want to get into Stanby's room later. If they do not have a key, they could get one."

"You might make a discreet inquiry about Lady Crieff while you are there," Hartley said.

Mott scowled. "Seems to me you are mighty interested in Lady Crieff. We ain't here to enjoy ourselves, Daniel."

"Any man with an eye in his head would be interested in her. 'Carpe diem' is my motto. Seize the day. You should always milk any situation for any enjoyment there is in it, Rudolph. If she is working with Stanby, she might prove useful—as well as amusing," he said, with a saturnine smile.

"Aye, and she might get her fingers into your wallet, too. What do you want for dinner?"

"Meat and potatoes."

"Damme, I have to know more than that. What shall I complain of? I want to sound as if I know what I am talking about."

"If it is beef, it is overdone. If it is fowl, it is tough as white leather. Improvise, Mott. You know what a fussy gourmet I am. The bully beef in Spain refines the palate to such an extent that even ambrosia does not entirely please me."

Mott left, and Hartly eventually undressed and took his bath. After several years fighting the French in Spain, he needed no assistance with his toilette. He had gone as a lieutenant and had been raised first to captain, then major, during the course of hard-fought battles. A man learned to do for himself in such rough circumstances as he had endured. His batman had been in the boughs at being left behind, but Hartly had felt it desirable to keep him on standby in case a new face was required later in the game. When Mott returned, he cast an approving eye over his cousin's black evening jacket and immaculate linens.

"I congratulate myself," Mott said. "I did a fine job of dressing you, Daniel. Lady Crieff will be impressed."

"Did you find out anything about her? Or Stanby?"

"Sally and Sukey—the servant girls—they are Bullion's daughters, by the by. They say Lady Crieff has never visited the Marchbanks. She is completely unknown hereabouts. As she just arrived, they have no way of knowing whether she is a friend of Stanby's. I did learn something about Sir David. He is her stepson."

"Stepson," Hartley said, frowning. "Yes, that is

possible. One assumes, then, that she married a gentleman considerably older than herself."

"And since the stepson is now Sir David, then obviously the husband is dead. Lady Crieff is a widow."

"Not for long, I warrant," Hartly said, with a pensive smile that set his cousin frowning in concern.

Hartly always had an eye for those raven-haired girls.

Chapter Three

Hartly was not so foolish as to imagine Bullion's Great Room would be as large as the average ballroom; the inn's size made it impossible. He did, however, anticipate something larger and grander than the dining room to which he was led when he went belowstairs to dinner. It was a low room approximately thirty feet square, which seemed considerably smaller, burdened as it was with scurrying servants, not less than six tables for four (each with accompanying chairs), two sideboards, and a fireplace with a settee fronting it. The walls were of rough, smoke-dimmed plaster and beams. Some strange, dark objects resembling giant bats suspended from the ceiling beams at irregular intervals. When he passed warily beneath one of those objects, he discovered it to be flowers hung to dry some decades previously, to judge by their brittleness.

Despite the room's crowded condition, it was pleasant enough. The blazing fire in the hearth cast a flickering light and warmth on the chamber. Voices rose in laughter and conversation from the occupied tables. The tantalizing smell of good roast beef fought with the gentler aroma of baking apples and cinnamon. A quick survey of the tables told Hartly that Lady Crieff's party had not yet arrived.

Bullion greeted his guests at the door. For the occasion of dinner in the Great Room, he had plastered his unruly hair down with grease and donned a jacket of brilliant blue, sporting yellow mohair buttons as big as saucers. With a wink and a nod, he led Hartly to a table and took his order. Hartly entertained himself with a surreptitious survey of the other guests until his dinner arrived. He had not spotted a likely candidate for Stanby, but two tables were empty. The other tables held family parties.

Abovestairs, Moira was preparing herself for her formal debut as Lady Crieff. She felt naked in the low-cut gown that displayed the upper portion of her bosoms in a wanton manner. Yet this was the pattern shown in *La Belle Assemblée* as being the latest mode in London, and Lady Crieff would surely be au courant in matters of toilette. Her silky hair did not take kindly to the intricate arrangement suggested in *La Belle Assemblée*. By dint of wetting it and curling it in papers, it had assumed an unfamiliar set of corkscrew curls that was so unattractive, Moira had pulled it all back from her face and held it with a ribbon.

"What do you think?" she asked Jonathon, when he came to accompany her down to dinner.

"You look like a lightskirt," he said bluntly. "But

a very pretty one. Stanby will certainly try to scrape an acquaintance."

"I shall flirt and giggle and act the vulgar fool. You must try not to laugh, Jonathon. This is extremely serious business."

Excitement lent a flush to her ivory skin and a glitter to her silvery eyes. Her heart pounded tumultuously as she took Jonathon's arm for the descent to the Great Room.

A hush fell over the dining room when she entered. Glancing to the doorway, Hartly observed it was the arrival of Lady Crieff's party that caused it. He displayed neither pleasure nor curiosity when they were shown to the table next to his own. His eyes did not rest transfixed on the young lady's ivory face, nor did they wander in a leisurely manner from her raven curls over her lithe waist to her dainty kid slippers. Yet without ogling in any obvious way, he had taken a close inventory of her charms. He decided that her mulberry velvet gown had been chosen to add to her years and make it appear less ludicrous that she had a stepson nearly as old as herself. The richly colored gown set off her pale satin skin to great advantage. He caught a tantalizing peep of the incipient swell of bosoms as she was seated. A modest set of diamonds sparkled at her throat. They were the only modest thing about her toilette, for the gown had a vulgar quantity of ribbons and lace. The lady's face was a visual delight, though. He cocked an ear to overhear what the party had to say.

"What wine shall we have, David?" she asked, in the voice of a young girl trying to sound experienced.

"I should like champagne," the young fellow announced.

"We shall have claret," Lady Crieff said. "And you are not to guzzle it. You know your papa would dislike to see you fuddled."

Hartly could not hear Sir David's reply. Jonathon said in a low voice, "I do not think Stanby is here, but Hartly has noticed us. P'raps you should ogle him a little."

Hartly finished his roast beef and had another sip of wine. It was not until Lady Crieff's party had ordered their dinner that he glanced that way again. Lady Crieff was studying him with sharp interest. She allowed her eyes to play with his a moment across the room before turning away. She whispered something to the lad. There was a flurry of low talk, after which Lady Crieff paid attention to her dinner for a few moments. E'er long, her wicked eyes slid to Hartly again. She was definitely flirting now, using her handsome eyes in a very practiced way. She did not stare but glanced shyly, looked away, then glanced again, with a fleeting, tantalizing smile that displayed a delightful set of dimples.

When another guest arrived, Moira abandoned Hartly to examine the newcomer. She saw a gentleman of military cut, who strode in as if he owned the place. He was of middle years, about fifty, but with a still youthful air about him. He had a good complexion, most of his own brown hair, and wore a well-cut black evening jacket. Her whole body stiffened. Her breaths came in shallow gasps, and her fork fell to her plate with a gentle clatter.

"It is Lionel March," she said in a low voice to Jonathon.

"Are you certain?"

"Positive."

"Your usual table, Major Stanby," Bullion said, ushering the newcomer to a table across the room. Bullion nodded at Hartly behind Stanby's back to alert him to Stanby's arrival.

Moira tried not to stare, but as if her eyes had a will of their own, they kept turning to March. Here was the infamous scoundrel who had bilked her and Jonathon of their fortune, and a dozen other innocent people as well, if half the rumors one heard were true. She looked with interest to his hands and saw that the left hand holding the menu kept the smallest finger bent, no doubt to conceal that the tip was missing. She meant to verify the fact before he left the room.

Hartly ordered apple tart, cheddar cheese, and coffee and settled down for some discreet observing of his own. Having ascertained Stanby's identity, he let his gaze wander again to Lady Crieff's table, where the mood had turned noticeably tense. She had given a start of alarm when Major Stanby entered. Now she looked as if she were dancing on coals. Her face was pale as paper. Did Stanby have some hold over her? The glazed look in her eyes was fear. Daniel had seen enough of it in his young soldiers in the Peninsula to recognize it. Fear and loathing. If she was indeed working with Stanby, she was not doing it willingly. His interest quickened.

He noticed that young Sir David displayed a monstrous interest in Stanby. What was he staring at? Hartly followed the line of his gaze and saw that Stanby had at last revealed the interesting digit. He was just taking up his fork, and for a brief instant, the small finger showed its mutilation.

It hardly accounted for the young lad's triumphant smile, or the way he poked his stepmama. His words were not audible, but as Lady Crieff's eyes immediately flew to Stanby's left hand, it was obvious what had been said. Was it merely childish curiosity at this irregularity that had caught Sir David's interest? If they were cohorts of Stanby, they would have been aware of it sooner.

"It is him!" Jonathon whispered. "I saw the finger."

"I told you it was. I have not a single doubt of it. His hair is lighter, and he has added a few pounds, but it is certainly March. I could never be mistaken about those eyes."

They were a dull cabbage green, with a sly look in them. If he had any lashes, they were colorless. Moira was unprepared for the storm of emotions that washed over her upon seeing her enemy again. It brought back the awful desolation following her mother's death, and the final injury of learning he had run off with the family fortune. She wanted to jump up and attack him physically as he sat calmly sipping his wine. It would take every ounce of her self-control to smile at this demon and pretend she did not hate him. But whatever it took, she would do it.

Her eyes moved to Hartly. He had just finished his apple tart and sat back, sipping his coffee, quite ignoring Stanby. Hartly looked well satisfied with his dinner. Moira could not even remember what she had eaten. Glancing at her plate, she saw that the tender, pink roast beef, Yorkshire pudding, and peas had hardly been tasted. What a waste—and she had paid a pretty penny for that dinner. Her whole enterprise was being run on a shoestring; she had no pennies to spare.

Her mind soon turned to more interesting things. At last she had run Lionel March to ground, and her next step was to make contact with him. She had to draw his attention in some manner. It was time for Lady Crieff to begin cutting up.

"This wine is quite horrid," she announced in a clear, carrying voice, pushing her glass away.

"Let us have champagne," Sir David suggested once more.

"Certainly not. It is much too—you are much too young," she replied.

Hartly, listening, wondered about that speech. It is much too—what? Champagne was not stronger than claret. But it was a deal more expensive. Were the Crieffs not so wealthy as the title suggested? The carriage they arrived in had been old but of good quality. The team of four was stout and well matched. The youngsters were rigged out in the highest kick of fashion, yet they traveled without servants. That was deuced odd. The girl at least ought to have a woman.

The young servant called Wilf, a slender boy with red hair, appeared at Hartly's elbow. "Could I bring you another bottle, sir?" he asked.

"No, I am finished. But perhaps the lady would like a bottle of my private stock," he said, indicating Moira. "I fear she is not happy with your wine. My man has had a dozen bottles placed with you. Pray give one to the lady, with my compliments."

The wine was duly delivered to the table. Moira's instinct was to reject it. She had to make her decision quickly. She could either accept, and further the acquaintance with Hartly, or she could refuse it, and make an enemy of him. Worse, she would give March the notion she was not approachable. She felt Lady Crieff would accept and cause a fuss by bringing Hartly to her table. That would get March's attention. She looked at the wine, then at Hartly. She nodded and smiled her acceptance with great condescension.

"Pray ask the gentleman if he would care to join us for a glass of his wine," she said to Wilf.

Hartly did not bother with the charade of pretending he had not heard her, thus requiring Wilf to repeat the message. He rose and went to the table, bowed, and said, "How very kind of you, ma'am, but I have already finished dinner and am having coffee. I overheard your complaint of Bullion's wine. I take the precaution of traveling with my own. I am Daniel Hartly, by the by."

"What a clever idea, Mr. Hartly! Why did we not bring our own from Penworth Hall, David? I am sure Sir Aubrey's cellar was always well stocked. Oh, you have not met my stepson, Mr. Hartly. Sir David Crieff." Jonathon bowed. "And I am Lady Crieff," she added, with a little laugh. "David's stepmama! Is it not ridiculous? Of course, Sir Aubrey was decades older than I. Which is not to say I married him for his blunt," she added firmly.

"There is no need to inquire why the late Sir Aubrey married you, Lady Crieff," Hartly replied, as his eyes wandered over her face, and lower to enjoy a quick appreciation of her bosoms. He saw there was no need for subtlety. The lovely lady, alas, was as common as dirt.

"Oh, fie!" She smiled, flapping her fingers at him. "I wager you say that to all the ladies, Mr. Hartly."

"No indeed! Only to the married ones whose beauty merits it."

"Now there is a handsome compliment indeed. I see you will want watching, sir."

While she chattered, a part of her mind was running in a different direction. Hartly had wasted no time rushing to meet her. He seemed intent on emptying the butter boat on her. Was his aim merely to seduce a young widow, or was he playing a deeper game, one that involved Lionel March?

Hartly bowed. "I shall try to behave. I am charmed to make your acquaintance—at last."

"At last?" she asked, frowning. "Why, you sound as if—"

"Every minute seems an hour when one awaits a treat," he said, coming to her rescue. Hartly expected a simpering smile at this trite compliment and was surprised to see a flash of amusement instead. Amusement and intelligence. By God, the hoyden was laughing at him. "Are you staying long at Owl House Inn?" he asked.

"A few days. It depends. And you, Mr. Hartly?"

"That also depends, madam."

Moira was disconcerted by his manner. His mischievous eyes suggested that his stay depended on how long she remained. She forced herself to play the flirt. Lady Crieff had not won a gouty squire twice her age by being backward, and she had to play her role to the hilt.

She allowed her long eyelashes to flutter coquettishly. "On what does it depend, Mr. Hartly, if I am not being too indiscreet to inquire?"

"On whether I find the company hereabouts congenial, ma'am," he responded, gazing boldly into her eyes, until her cheeks felt warm. "I hope I have found one friend, at least," he added.

"I hope so indeed. We shall see whether flattery is the quickest path to friendship."

Hartly said what was expected of him: "Flattery?" He went on to assure her in a voice of silken insincerity that it had been no such thing.

"Will you not bring your coffee to our table, sir?" she said. "I swear my neck is developing a crick, having to look up at you. It seems so uncivil, does it not, eating in a room with all these tables, and no one speaking to anyone else? What is the good of putting up at an inn if one is not to meet new gentle—new people?" She allowed her lashes to flutter enticingly.

"The perils of travel." He nodded. "One dislikes to be standoffish, yet to force an acquaintance seems just a touch vulgar. I opted for vulgarity. I should be honored to join you."

Wilf, who had been listening shamelessly to this exchange, darted off for the coffee. Hartly sat in the vacant chair between Sir David and Lady Crieff.

Lady Crieff tried the wine and said, "I congratulate you on your taste. This is quite as good as what comes out of Sir Aubrey's cellar. Are you from these parts, Mr. Hartly?"

"No, from Devon. I am on holiday. I shall be going on to London to visit relatives when the spirit moves me."

She sighed. "How nice to be a footloose bachelor." She let her voice rise a notch to indicate interest. "Or perhaps I am taking too much for granted to assume you are not married?" she asked.

"I am a bachelor. And where are you folks from?"

"Scotland."

"I own a great big sheep farm in the Moorfoot Hills," Sir David boasted. "P'raps you have heard of it—Penworth Hall?"

"No, I have never been to Scotland. I hear it is beautiful. How large a flock do you have, Sir David?"

"Hundreds," he said, looking helplessly to Lady Crieff.

"Ninnyhammer," she scolded. "Sir David has over a thousand sheep, Mr. Hartly. And two thousand acres," she added, choosing numbers that sounded impressive without stretching the bounds of credibility. The journals had stated only that Penworth Hall was a large, prosperous estate.

She turned to Sir David. "And it is high time you informed yourself of your estate, David. It is all yours, now that your papa has stuck his fork in the wall. I, alas, got only—but Mr. Hartly is not interested in me," she said, with a coquettish glance.

The incident raised a doubt in Hartly's mind. Odd that a lad of sixteen or so years was unaware of the extent of his holdings. He would get him alone soon and give him a more thorough quizzing. It also raised the question—what had Lady Crieff got? She had been carrying a padlocked case, presumably of jewels. He looked at the diamond necklace at her throat. It was modest but genuine. Iridescent prisms glowed in its depths when she moved. They danced over the satin mounds of her breasts, which just peeped over the top of her gown. When she noticed where he was looking, she gave him a knowing smile, then pulled her shawl over her bosom.

"My own estate specializes in cattle," he said. "Have you seen anything of the neighborhood yet?"

He pitched his question between the two, for he wanted to include the young lad in any outing.

"We just arrived this afternoon," Lady Crieff replied. "It seems a desolate enough place. Not a decent shop to be seen. I daresay there are no assemblies at Blaxstead?"

"Like you, I have just arrived. We arrived at the same time, I believe," he mentioned. "I plan to drive about the neighborhood tomorrow to see what entertainments offer. Might I induce you to join me?"

"Now, that is what I call neighborly, Mr. Hartly. I should like it, of all things!" Lady Crieff replied, but she accepted with an air of conferring a favor and went on to add that David must accompany them. "Not that I mean to say I mistrust you, but for the looks of it, you know. I shall be happy to go. I am not one to look down on a fellow just because he does not have a handle to his name. I invited every gentleman who owned a decent jacket to my routs at Penworth. I have had over a hundred in the ballroom at one time, have I not, David? I try to round up a few spare gents, you must know, so the plainer girls do not have to sit on their haunches all evening."

"How exceedingly considerate of you," Hartly replied, chewing back a grin.

She smiled her pleasure. "Everyone said I had the best parties in the neighborhood. Mind you, Sir Aubrey was not too fond of them, but I could always get around *him*."

"I wager you could."

Hartly was happy that David interrupted the conversation, for he hardly knew how to converse with such a vulgar piece of merchandise. Were it not for the suspicion that she had something to do with Stanby, he would have left long ago. He felt a rankling annoyance that her beauty was spoiled by her common manners and self-seeking ways.

"Can I drive your curricle?" Sir David asked.

"I am afraid my team would be a bit much for you to handle. Well, folks, it is settled then that you will join me tomorrow, if the weather is fine?"

Moira began wondering why Mr. Hartly was so insistent on furthering the acquaintance. She was sharp enough to see he had no good opinion of her as a person. His original admiration had turned to disparagement once she went into her act. Laughing up his sleeve, if the truth were known. He had been examining her diamonds in a troublesome way, and he had been asking for Major Stanby earlier.

"Let us wait and see if the weather is good," she said.

"There speaks the voice of caution," Hartly replied, concealing his annoyance behind a smile. "I shall pray for sunshine."

He was too wise to rush his fences, nor was it necessary. The pretty vixen was interested in him. He finished his coffee and took his leave, after expressing his pleasure in making their acquaintance. He had a fair idea where they would go after dinner. The evening light lingered long in May. The inn offered no entertainment, and with boredom and water to lure them outside, he figured he would meet up with the pair again on the banks of the estuary. His real interest was in scraping an acquaintance with Stanby. With this end in view, he spoke to Bullion in a raised voice on his way out.

"Any chance of a game of cards later this evening, Bullion?" he asked.

"We usually have a friendly game in a corner of the room. A bunch of the local lads drop in about nine." He nodded knowingly to Stanby. "A few of my guests sit down as well."

"Excellent. I shall do likewise. A fine dinner. I particularly enjoyed your Cook's apple tart."

"Sorry about the bread sauce. Your man was asking for it, but my Maggie don't care for outsiders in her kitchen. She'll make it for you herself tomorrow in place of the Yorkshire. How is that, then?"

"Mott has a strange idea of what I like! I despise bread sauce. Pay him no heed."

Bullion smiled in satisfaction. Why was it the servants of the mighty were so much more demanding than their masters?

"My Maggie'll be happy to hear it."

Hartly went out into the cool evening, surprised that it was still twilight. It had seemed like the middle of the night in the Great Room.

Chapter Four

As soon as Hartly left the room, Moira said to her brother, "He wasted no time in putting himself forward."

"He was ogling the diamonds," Jonathon said. "I should sleep with them under my pillow if I were you."

Moira's eyes kept darting to Major Stanby as she ate her apple tart. "*He* shows no interest. He cannot know who Lady Crieff is. We must leak the details of her history to him somehow. Hartly had no notion of it either. I had thought she was infamous enough to be known by name. I shall leave the clippings from the journals on my bedside table. No doubt the servants will read them and spread the word. Or you could let it slip tomorrow," she suggested. "It is the sort of thing a youngster might be foolish enough to boast of."

"I ain't exactly a youngster," he exclaimed, taking instant objection to the charge.

"Only in years," she said sadly. "You have had to

grow up fast, and without the sort of education you deserve, though the vicar did a fine job of tutoring you. You will finish your education at Eton or Harrow when we get our money back, then go on to university, as Papa wanted."

"I do not care a brass farthing for that. It is you who deserves a treat after this is over—if we can get our money back, I mean."

"We'll do it, David," she said firmly. "Never allow yourself to doubt. It would be the beginning of the end. If we failed, we would have to go on living as we have been—perhaps even lose the Elms. We have found him." Her eyes slid to Lionel March. "The job is half-done, and we will finish it."

When they left, Major Stanby was still at the table.

"It is only eight o'clock," Jonathon said, as they left the room. "Let us go out for a stroll before it comes on dark, Lady Crieff. It will be a long evening, locked up in our rooms."

"You have not forgotten that Lady Marchbank is sending her footman over to see that we arrived safe and sound, and arrange a time for us to call?" Moira replied.

"We shall see her carriage when it arrives. Do let us go out," Jonathon urged.

"Very well, but we cannot stray far from the inn."

When they stepped outside, the air held the clammy moisture and scent of the sea. The setting sun cast a crimson net over the dark water. A few fishing boats bobbed at anchor. A grass bank ran down to the estuary, ending in a bed of rushes. The estuary curved in an arc around Owl Point. At the end of the point sat Owl House Inn, backing on the water. Moira thought it a most desolate scene, after the lush richness of Surrey. At the rear of the inn, where a wharf protruded into the water, a fishing smack was unloading its catch.

A few of the locals and inn patrons were strolling along the bank. It was not long before Moira spotted Mr. Hartly. He was at the rear of the inn, talking to a man David identified as his valet. David had made a few trips belowstairs during the afternoon and castigated Mott as a man milliner.

Hartly saw the Crieffs but did not rush forward to greet them. He had espied a more interesting person: Major Stanby had just come out of the inn and was gazing at the water. When he spotted Hartly, he began sauntering toward the rear of the inn.

"Here he comes now," Hartly said to Mott. "I hoped that mention of a card game would draw him out."

Moira noticed where Stanby was going. "I knew it!" she exclaimed. "They *are* acquainted. Run along and pretend you are looking at the fish, David, and tell me what is said."

Jonathon was always happy to perform any chore that had an air of wickedness about it. He darted off, ostensibly to watch the unloading of the boat. Mott had left. Neither Hartly nor Stanby paid him any heed.

E'er long, Jonathon was back. "A card game," he said. "Tonight, in the Great Room. They pretended they did not know each other to fool me."

"I do not think they even saw you," Moira replied, frowning. "What can Hartly be up to? I shall go to the Great Room to read and see what happens."

Even while she spoke, the gentlemen turned and

began to walk toward the front of the inn. Hartly smiled when he saw her. If the lady was innocent, he had no wish to bring Stanby down on her head, yet he was eager to see how they behaved together.

"That is Lady Crieff," he mentioned as they walked along. "Do you know her?"

"Lady Crieff? The name sounds familiar." Something in Stanby's tone caught Hartly's attention. The man was staring at her with a deep frown between his eyebrows, as if trying to remember. Then he shook his head in frustration. "No, that is not a face a gentleman would forget in a hurry. Beautiful! Is she a friend of yours?"

"A new acquaintance."

When Moira saw that the gentlemen were coming toward her, she felt a nearly overwhelming urge to flee. She could never carry her scheme off. She had held her grudge against Lionel March too long to smile and greet him with politeness. Yet it was crucial to her plan that she not only meet him but become close enough that she confide in him her need to sell her jewelry. She took a deep breath and prepared herself for her first exchange of words with Lionel March in four years.

Before she had time for more misgivings, Hartly came forward and introduced Major Stanby to her and David. To avoid having to take his hand, Moira made a stiff curtsy. Sir David played his part with credit. It helped that Stanby was wearing gloves. She knew her brother could not prevent himself from staring at that finger if his hands had been bare.

The ensuing conversation was trite to the point of banality. Hartly noticed that Lady Crieff's demeanor had changed dramatically from their dinner meeting. She did not flirt or act the hoyden. In fact, she was nearly inarticulate—and again that fear and loathing were in her eyes, though she tried to conceal it.

She mentioned the beauty of the evening, and each discovered of the other where they were from. Major Stanby claimed to hail from the Lake District in the north of England, a good, safe distance from their present location.

"Perhaps you are familiar with it, Lady Crieff, as you are from neighboring Scotland?" he asked in an avuncular way.

"Alas, only a glimpse on our way south. We never strayed far from the Great North Road. One hears it is lovely. I should like to pay a proper visit sometime and see the lake made famous by the poets."

"Ah, yes, Lake Windermere. You really should—on your way home, perhaps?" His voice made it a question.

Windermere? But it was Grasmere where Wordsworth and Coleridge lived. "I am not returning to Scotland," Lady Crieff said. "I plan to live in London."

"Indeed!" His exclamation was a virtual request for more information. Moira noticed that Mr. Hartly also looked curious to hear more.

"Sir David will return to Penworth Hall, of course. The estate was entailed on him when my husband died last year. We decided to give him a little holiday in London first."

"You have friends—relatives—in London, of course," Stanby said.

"Yes," she replied, without expanding. "And some

business to transact there as well, to settle the estate."

"Will you remain long here at the inn?" Stanby asked, with the keenest interest.

"Actually, I am to meet someone here. A friend." She had made the initial contact with March, and her nerves were so shattered that she wanted only to run upstairs and recuperate. She would do better another time, after she had got over the first shock. It was his gooseberry eyes, especially, that caused that deep sense of revulsion. "We really ought to be going in now, David," she said. "It is coming on dark."

Mr. Hartly was curious at her changed manner. Where were the coy glances, the come-hither smiles, the common streak that had been so pronounced earlier? It seemed the lady was putting on a show of gentility for Stanby.

"A wise precaution," Stanby agreed.

A frozen smile moved her lips. "There is no saying who might be putting up at a place like this. I had planned to stay with my cousin, Lady Marchbank. She lives nearby at Cove House. She wanted us to put up with her, but as her husband is ailing, I did not think it was the proper time to intrude."

She and Jonathon took their leave and went into the inn.

"We could have stayed a little longer," Jonathon chided. "Why did you not say something about the jewelry?"

"Let him find out things by degrees. It would look odd to be telling too much to strangers."

Stanby watched them as they returned to the inn. When they entered, he lifted an eyebrow at Hartly. "Lady Crieff is a little young to be jaunting about the countryside without a proper chaperon. Not quite *comme il faut*, do you not think?"

"It is difficult to say, on such short acquaintance."

"I could not help overhearing some of her conversation with you at dinner, Hartly. A bit of a dasher, I thought." His green eyes were bright with curiosity.

"That was my impression. Yet if she is related to the Marchbanks, one must assume she is respectable."

"Yes, *if*," Stanby said, with a disparaging sniff.

They were still talking by the estuary when a black carriage with the nobleman's crest on the door arrived at the inn.

"That would be Lady Marchbank's rig," Stanby said, examining it closely. "It seems there is some connection between the ladies after all. But then, you know, some of the county nobility is no better than it should be. Shall we go in and begin that game of cards?"

Hartly was surprised to see Lady Crieff and Sir David occupying the settee in front of the grate. They paid no attention to the card players, however. The inn was so informal that a few other ladies were also making use of the Great Room, as an alternative to retiring to their small chambers so early. Lady Crieff was thumbing idly through the journals. After ten minutes, Sir David rose and sauntered closer to the card table to listen to the conversation.

The card game with the locals was for small stakes, and friendly in nature. Over the space of two hours, Hartly won a few guineas. When Stanby suggested they get together for a "more interesting game" another time, he agreed. It was an old trick:

to allow a victim to win a small sum to put him at his ease and feel safe playing for higher stakes another time. Stanby had done a little discreet questioning to discover how deep his partner's pockets were, and Hartly had painted himself as a young provincial with more money than brains.

They were just about to leave the table when a new guest entered. Moira glanced up to see who was arriving so late at night. The man wore a drab driving coat with not less than a dozen collars. Once the coat was removed, he stood revealed as a slender fellow. He had not changed into evening clothes, but his well-cut jacket, his intricate cravat, and his blond hair, brushed forward in the Brutus do, proclaimed him a very tulip of fashion.

"I say, not breaking up the game so early?" he exclaimed. "It is only eleven bells. Damn, split open another bottle and let us have a few hands. I have just arrived from London with my pockets bulging. Won a thousand off Lord Felsham last night. Forced to rusticate a while. Did I introduce myself? I am Ponsonby. Killed my man this morning at dawn," he boasted. "That will teach him to impugn the name of Ponsonby. Bow Street is after me. If they send one of their runners creeping about, you have not seen me. There's a good fellow." He reached out and patted Stanby on the shoulder. "I don't believe I caught your name."

"Major Stanby, and this is Hartly. I have had enough cards for one evening," Stanby said, "but if you would care to join Hartly and myself, we will be playing tomorrow evening."

"That's a dashed long time to wait. Still, there are other amusements, eh? How are the serving wenches here? Are they pretty?"

"They are the innkeeper's daughters," Stanby replied. "I would not meddle with them if I were you."

"Damn, what sort of Methodist inn have I wandered into? I shall drive on tomorrow."

"What a good idea," Hartly murmured. Ponsonby had not observed Lady Crieff, but Hartly feared that once he did, he would become obstreperous.

"Dashed odd thing, by God," Ponsonby continued. "I heard the Owl served the best brandy in England, and here I find you drinking this catlap." He wrinkled his nose at the glasses of ale on the table. "Thought I might take a keg or two back with me, what? Treat the lads. Where is mein host? Bullion! Bullion, I say. Brandy for me and my friends. We shall drink a bumper to Noddy. Did I tell you I killed him? Well, nicked him, at least. Daresay he will stick his fork in the wall. Just like the gudgeon."

Bullion came scurrying forward. "Hush now, sir," he said to Ponsonby. "I can let you have a drop, but you must not be so clamorous about it. It's agin the law, you see."

"Fie on the law! Bring on the brandy."

Bullion disappeared and soon returned to place a bottle on the table. Ponsonby poured for them all and proposed a toast to Noddy.

"This is excellent stuff!" Stanby exclaimed, after tasting it. "By God, I have not had such fine brandy in a twelvemonth. I shall take a keg of this away with me when I leave."

Bullion stood, smiling at his guests. "We get the real thing here, gentlemen. That fishing boat you saw unloading at twilight—this batch was buried under the mackerel. We get her fresh from France, before the adulterers get at it with their caramel and water."

"Ho ho! Adulterers, eh?" Ponsonby said, with a loose-lipped smile. "Where are the wenches? Bring on the wenches."

"It is not that sort of adulterer Bullion speaks of," Stanby explained. "It refers to diluting the brandy." He turned to Bullion. "I should like a hogshead of this myself. Could you put me in touch with the leader, Bullion?"

Bullion stared at him in wide-eyed amazement. "That is more than my life would be worth, sir. No one knows the ringleader. Hereabouts he is called the Black Ghost. A gentleman, all dressed in black, even including a mask over his face, has been spotted flying through the night from time to time, but no one is foolish enough to accost him. He would slit the throat of anyone who saw his face. Smuggling is a capital crime, so he takes no chances. Mind you, it pays well."

Ponsonby poured the innkeeper a glass of brandy, and after a sip, the innkeeper continued his discourse.

"They do say the Blaxstead run is the most profitable one in the kingdom, bar none. There's highly placed folks in on it," Bullion told them, with a wise nod of his head. "Stands to reason, don't it? I mean to say, never an arrest in ten years. The Potter lads, Joe and Jim, hired as Revenuemen. The whole Potter family is simple. Looks as though someone high up don't want the Gentlemen caught. But that is not for me to say. Oh, no, I could not put you in touch with the *leader*, but I am on terms with the Gentlemen. That is what we call the smugglers hereabouts. They supply my needs, for a certain consideration. How many barrels will you be wanting then, sir?"

Stanby and Ponsonby both gave an order for two each. Hartly said, "As I am on holiday, I do not fancy carrying contraband to London, then all the way back to Devon. I shall pass, reluctantly. It is excellent stuff."

Bullion left, and the three gentlemen sat on at the table, enjoying their brandy.

"That must be a profitable concession, the brandy running here in Blaxstead," the major said. "I should not mind investing in it. Safe as churches, if the local authorities are being paid to cooperate. I wonder who this mysterious Black Ghost is. The local lord, perhaps?"

"It is best not to interfere with the Gentlemen," Ponsonby said firmly. "My friend, the Duke of Mersey, tried to run them off his beach. His dower house burned down the next night. He took the hint. The Gentlemen do not fool around. And that was only a small smuggling gang. Here at Blaxstead it stands to reason they would be vicious." He shivered and took another sip.

"I wonder if he would be interested in taking on a partner, though," Stanby said. "Add another ship or two to his fleet. I happen to have a good bit of cash standing idle at the moment from my operations in Canada."

Hartly came to rigid attention; so did Ponsonby, though no one noticed it.

Stanby continued, "I was there during the war of '12. Before leaving the country, I bought up certain tracts of lumber and some fur-trading routes. They have proved profitable. What I miss is the excitement of soldiering. I should not mind taking a small active part in the Black Ghost's operation."

"Ah, my good sir, you are an ossifer and a gen'leman," Ponsonby said, becoming noticeably bosky. "Is that where you got your finger chopped off—in Canada?" He stared at the finger, his blue eyes glazed with drink. "No harm to ask, eh? Odd-looking thing, like a little bald head. Heh heh."

"I wish I could say an Indian took it off with an arrow," the major replied, "but it was nothing so heroic. It got frostbitten and became infected. The sawbones felt there was some danger of gangrene, with a possibility of losing the whole hand. In the wilds of Canada, as we were, there were no proper hospital facilities, so the doctor did not want to operate. 'Chop it off!' I told him. 'It will not stop me from using my Brown Bess.' Nor did it."

Ponsonby listened as one entranced. "You are a hero, Major. 'Chop it off!' By God, that could not have been pleasant."

"I was one of the fortunate ones," the major said modestly. "Others lost a whole limb."

Moira listened, her lips curled cynically. He had told Mama he got his finger caught in a mantrap, while releasing a young boy who had straggled into it. It had probably been shot off by someone who had caught him dealing shaved cards. His vanity invented these heroic feats to impress his listeners.

"You have led a life of action," Ponsonby said wistfully, "while I have lingered in the fleshpots of Babylon. I say, lads, this smuggling—there would be the life, eh? On the open seas."

Hartly listened closely, without commenting. The item of major interest to him was that Stanby's pockets were full—that was good news. If it proved impossible to relieve Stanby of fifteen thousand at cards, he might put this smuggling business to some use. It would not be hard to pose as the Black Ghost, a gentleman no one had ever seen. Or Gibbs, his batman, could do it. Stanby was no flat, however. He would want proof that he was getting his money's worth before turning over fifteen thousand pounds to anyone, even the Black Ghost.

During a lull in the conversation, Hartly rose and announced his intention of retiring.

Ponsonby staggered to his feet to bid him farewell. "Run along, then," he said, his loose smile stretching wide. "Major Shtanby and I have business to discush. Damn, stand still. Why are you weaving—" He happened to glance to the grate and espied Moira sitting quietly there, reading. He froze to the spot, like a pointer on the scent of game. "By Jove!" he exclaimed. "Now there is what I call a comely wench!"

Chapter Five

Ponsonby began to stagger in her direction. "A wench! By God, I shall have a warm bed tonight."

Moira looked up, her eyes wide with interest. "Go away!" she said firmly, as he fell onto the sofa beside her. "David!"

Jonathon gamely put his hand on Ponsonby's shoulder. "I say, old man. You had best move on. This is Lady Crieff."

"And I, sir, am an oss—no, that is the major. I am someone important. I remember that much." His bleary gaze turned to devour Moira. "By God, you are a beauty, madam. Will you marry me?" He reached out and grasped her shoulders, while Jonathon struggled to pull him away.

Hartly and Stanby moved in and took hold of him.

"It might be best if you leave, Lady Crieff," Stanby said. "Ponsonby is a trifle disguised." He turned to Hartly. "You accompany Lady Crieff to her room, Hartly. Bullion and I will see that Ponsonby gets to bed."

It occurred to Hartly that Sir David could accompany Lady Crieff safely upstairs. The lady did not suggest it, however. She turned her sparkling eyes on Hartly and said, "What riffraff one meets in a place like this. Thank heaven there is one gentleman present."

"Lady Crieff?" he said, offering her his arm.

"My hero!" She laughed and placed her dainty fingers on his arm.

"I am the one who held Ponsonby off!" Jonathon exclaimed indignantly.

"So you did. Run along, David," she said, dismissing him without a word of thanks. "It is past your bedtime."

Jonathon appeared accustomed to doing as he was told. He ran upstairs without arguing.

Lady Crieff turned a flirtatious smile on her hero. "I should not have stayed in the Great Room," she said, "but it was so lonely and boring in my room, with nothing to do. And it is not as though I were a young deb. I was a married lady for three years. As a widow, I am allowed some leeway, do you not think, Mr. Hartly?"

"Certainly, madam, but perhaps a little discretion is advised in future. The other ladies left the room an hour ago."

She made a moue, while gazing invitingly into his eyes. "You think I am horrid. It is very lonesome being a widow, Mr. Hartly," she said. "I had to watch my p's and q's at Penworth Hall. You have no idea how the old cats squeal if you look sideways at a gentleman. But I had thought that here I might be a little freer."

They reached her door. Moira was eager to escape, but she doubted that Lady Crieff would dismiss a handsome young gentleman so swiftly. Besides, this was a perfect opportunity to quiz him a little, to discover what he was up to.

"Would you think I was very fast if I invited you into my sitting room for a glass of wine, Mr. Hartly? David will be in the next room. We could leave the door open."

Hartly assumed the lady was open for dalliance. A widow, after all, and not a very cautious one, to judge by her behavior. "If you promise you won't seduce me, Lady Crieff," he replied, with a rakish smile that made a mockery of the words.

She said archly, "Why, Mr. Hartly! I would not have the least notion how to set about it, I promise you."

"Pity," he murmured.

Moira gave a nervous gurgle of laughter and unlocked the door. The lamps were burning in the sitting room. A bottle of wine and glasses sat on the sofa table beside the grate. She made a commotion about unlocking David's door, but Hartly noticed she did not actually leave it open.

"I shall be right in here with Mr. Hartly, David," she said. "We shan't disturb you. Do not forget to brush your teeth. Sleep tight, dear."

Then she went to the sofa. Hartly had already poured the wine. He lifted his glass in a toast. "That is that!" she said, and sat down beside him. "I try to be a mother to the boy, since he has lost his papa. He is a good lad. Not terribly bright, you know, but good-hearted."

"And discreet, I trust?" he asked, glancing to the closed door.

She gave a coy glance. "Whatever can you mean,

Mr. Hartly? I am sure I would never do anything that would ruin my reputation."

"When you are in Scotland, you mean?"

She sniffed. Mr. Hartly was beginning to examine her in a predatory way. She decided it was time to begin her quizzing.

"What do you think of Major Stanby?" she asked in a casual manner.

"I know virtually nothing of the man. I met him only today. I do not think you need worry about him, but I should avoid having much to do with young Ponsonby if I were you."

Ponsonby was of no interest to her. "He has come far from home—the Lake District. Major Stanby, I mean."

"But not so far as yourself."

She bit her lip in uncertainty. She had no wish to show she doubted Stanby's account of himself, yet it would be interesting to hear what Hartly had to say about his blunder.

"It is odd that he does not know the lake made famous by the poets. It is Grasmere, not Windermere." She looked at Hartly. He just shrugged. "But then a major would not be much interested in poetry."

"And he has been out of the country besides," Hartly mentioned. Of more interest to him was that Lady Crieff had ever heard of the Lake poets. "Are you interested in poetry, Lady Crieff?"

She swiftly raked her mind to consider what Lady Crieff's views on poetry might be. "Sir Aubrey had no interest in poetry. Except for Robbie Burns," she added, naming the one Scottish poet that came to mind.

"But I was not speaking of your late husband; I was speaking of you," he said.

"Why, you must know it is a wife's duty to like what her husband likes, Mr. Hartly."

"Perhaps—while her husband is alive," he said, gazing into her silver eyes.

An air of tension began to build as the silence stretched between them. A dozen vague thoughts whirled through Hartly's mind. It was Stanby who had suggested he accompany Lady Crieff abovestairs. Was that a clumsy attempt to throw them together? Was the lady about to initiate some scheme to empty his pockets? It was odd she had mentioned Stanby's blunder if she was his accomplice. And Stanby had openly questioned her respectability as well.

"But Sir Aubrey, alas, is gone now," he said, reading her face for signs of her intentions. "And we are here."

"It is odd, our meeting here. And Standby putting up at a little out-of-the-way place like this as well," she added casually.

"You are forgetting Ponsonby," he said, going along with her. "A man must be someplace."

She did not want to incite Hartly to too much suspicion, so she said, "That is true. The reason I mention it . . . Well, the fact is, I am traveling with something of considerable value. I just wondered if you thought there was any risk from the major."

A warning bell rang inside his head. Why was she telling him this? Was the lady about to involve him in some shady business of her own, some business that had nothing to do with Stanby? He remembered her look of fear when the major had been introduced to her.

"Have you any reason to think so?" he asked.

Moira bit back her annoyance at his unhelpful response. "Not really. It is just the way he looks at me, with those horrid gooseberry eyes, saying all the right things but not meaning them."

"I think you are overly imaginative, Lady Crieff, but if you dislike the man, you need have nothing to do with him."

She let her head fall forward, then looked up at him shyly from the corners of her beautiful eyes. "I am glad you are here to protect me, Mr. Hartly."

Hartly considered it as good as an invitation. His arm reached out and went around her shoulder. He pulled her against his chest. Lord, but she was a beauty, with those deep silver pools of eyes and ripe cherry lips, just asking to be kissed. The creamy mounds of her full breasts strained against their velvet nest. As if by instinct, he raised his hand and placed it on her breast. She gave a convulsive leap.

"What are you doing, Mr. Hartly!" she exclaimed in a shocked whisper, though her voice was not raised, presumably to prevent David from hearing.

"Just what you invited me here to do, milady. Making love to you."

Without further ado, he crushed her against him and plundered those full, lush lips. He paid no heed when she made an attempt to free herself, taking it for a token resistance, to save face.

Moira felt helpless. She admitted it was at least partly her own fault, as she had invited Hartly into her room. She knew she was in no real danger, with Jonathon next door. She could make some commotion—shout or knock over a lamp—but she was not happy to let Jonathon see what was happening. Living quietly in the country, she had had no opportunity to discover the secrets of love. Naturally it was a matter that intrigued her deeply, and here was her chance to learn. It was not at all what she had imagined her first kiss being like. She had pictured a gentle embrace, perhaps by moonlight, with a tame lover asking permission.

Hartly's embrace was nothing like that. He did not ask; he took, and she found that, after all, that was the way an embrace should be. There should be a sense of compulsion to it. She stopped trying to push him away and gave herself over to the strange experience. Odd how lips pressing on lips sent those hot rushes of pleasure through the whole body. When Hartly moved one arm away, she did not rush to free herself but waited to see what he would do. She felt his fingers lightly brushing her cheek. It felt pleasant at first, but when his fingers began to slide down toward her breast, she drew them back up.

His lips continued nibbling at hers, murmuring husky endearments against her fevered cheek. "My God, you are a temptress, milady." His warm fingers found their way to the bodice of her gown but did not stray lower. "Your skin is like Devon cream, so lush and smooth."

Moira felt a stab of weakness invade her being. She was allowing Mr. Hartly unspeakable liberties. What would Lady Marchbank think if she ever found out? "You must not say such things, Mr. Hartly!" she said primly.

He lifted his head and gazed at her with wildly dilated eyes, which were like a glitter of dark sapphires. Then he lowered his head and kissed her again. She felt a flicker of moistness pressing insistently against her lips. What was he doing? She pulled away sharply. His arms went around her, pulling her more tightly against him until her soft breasts melded to his firm chest.

An inchoate gasp hovered on the air. In her state of perturbation, she was not sure whether it came from herself or Mr. Hartly. Her fingers rose to tangle in his crisp hair. She felt his strong hands drawing along the contours of her sides, measuring her small waist, lingering over the flare of hips.

When he lifted his head, he was breathing heavily, and his face was flushed. He was immensely relieved that she was only a lightskirt and nothing more.

"Is he asleep yet?" he asked in a ragged voice. "I cannot take much more of this. Let us go to your bedchamber. He will not hear through the sitting room. I want you now."

Moira drew back and blinked dumbly. "Mr. Hartly!" she said. "I hope you do not think I am that sort of girl!"

A bark of laughter erupted on the still air. "I know exactly what sort of girl you are, milady. Come, why waste time? Or is there a fee to be settled first? Is that it?"

"What . . . what do you mean?" she asked in perplexity.

"I mean do you charge for your services, or is this an exercise in mutual gratification? I have no objection either way."

"What services?" She blinked twice, then a mask of outrage seized her features. "Mr. Hartly! You had better leave at once."

"The hell I will. You brought me here. You have excited me beyond control."

He made a lunge for her. Moira leapt up and grabbed the poker. "Get out."

Hartly looked at her and saw the real anger sparking in her eyes. Those lips that had been so warmly inviting a moment ago were now firmed in determination.

"Well, well," he said satirically. "It was misleading for you to suggest Stanby should be watched, madam. It is women like you who ought to be banned from decent establishments."

Moira bit her underlip. There was some truth in what Mr. Hartly was implying. She had led him on, but she had not intended for it to go so far. Even she had nearly lost control, and from what her friends told her, gentlemen had a much harder time of it.

Her hand flew to her lips, and tears started in her eyes. "Oh, Mr. Hartly, whatever must you think of me? But I did not mean for it to happen. Indeed I did not." She gave a hiccup of fear. "I had no notion. . . . You must forgive me. You will not tell anyone?"

Hartly just stood, staring in confusion. It seemed impossible that a widow had so little notion how lovemaking proceeded on its inevitable course. Just how old had her husband been?

"I am not likely to boast of my failure," he said grimly.

"Failure? But . . . but it was rather enjoyable, was it not?" she asked uncertainly.

A rueful smile seized his lips. "So it was, madam. But when a man is shown an appetizing dish, he usually expects to do more than look at it. I suggest you bear it in mind in future. Good night."

He strode to the door and opened it.

"I am sorry, Mr. Hartly," she said in a small voice.

He stopped and looked back at her. Her fingers were raised to her lips. Her angry determination had changed to an appealing air of uncertainty. She looked about fifteen years old and as innocent as a maiden.

"So am I, Lady Crieff," he said with great feeling.

"Do you still want to take me and David for that drive tomorrow?"

He just looked at her, shaking his head in wonder. "Well, if that don't beat the Dutch," he said, and left.

He went straight to his room to ponder the strange interlude. A wanton widow had invited him to her chamber. She had welcomed his embraces, had shown every eagerness for his advances. Then suddenly she turned into an outraged female. And if that were not enough to confuse Solomon, she had apologized after and asked if he still wanted to see her tomorrow. He decided he must be as mad as Lady Crieff—because he was eager for their date.

After Hartly had thought about that odd episode, he began to feel some concern for Ponsonby, who had been bragging about his full pockets. Stanby might relieve him of that thousand pounds.

Mott came to the door of the adjoining room. "Well, what happened?" he asked.

Hartly had to think a moment before he realized Mott was inquiring about Stanby.

"He let me win a few pounds tonight," he replied. "We have a private game fixed for tomorrow night. That is when we'll make our move. A fellow called Ponsonby arrived. He was completely foxed." He told Mott about the man, adding his concern that Stanby might fleece him.

"I shall take a nip down and see he is all right," Mott said. "This troublesome master of mine wants a posset at half past midnight. A valet's work is never done."

He was just about to open the door when he heard someone walking briskly down the hall. He let the man pass, then opened the door a crack. Hartly went to take a peek as well. It was Ponsonby. He was not drunk at all but walking in a straight, purposeful way. Hartly was seized with the notion that he was heading for Lady Crieff's room. He watched, but Ponsonby continued past her door to his own room. Another mysterious guest at the Owl House Inn.

Chapter Six

By morning, word of Lady Crieff's interesting history had begun to seep out. Moira did not see how it was possible, for the maids had not been in to read the clippings, but she knew it as soon as they entered the Great Room for breakfast. All eyes turned to her; after the first telltale hush, a low murmur broke out.

Major Stanby, who was just leaving the room, bowed and said, "Good morning, Lady Crieff, Sir David," with a new warmth. "A lovely day. I hear Bullion is having a small rout party this evening here in the Great Room. Not what you are accustomed to at Penworth, but perhaps you will honor us with your presence?"

"A party! I should love it, of all things!" she replied.

"You will save a dance for me?"

"But of course, Major. I look forward to it."

"Can I go?" Jonathon asked eagerly. "You know Papa said I could when I turned sixteen, Lady Crieff."

"Lawks, you are much too young. But then there will be no one here to see. Oh, Major! How shocking of me. *You* will be here," she said, simpering. "But you will forgive me if I am a trifle lenient with the lad. We have both had such a dull scald of it since Sir Aubrey died that we are eager for a little fling."

"No harm in it." The major smiled leniently. "With such rakes as Ponsonby present, you will require Sir David as a chaperon."

"I ain't a chaperon!" Jonathon exclaimed. "That is ladies' work. I am Lady Crieff's escort." On that bold speech he took Moira's arm and led her to the table.

Mr. Ponsonby was not slow to approach them. "I come hanging my head in shame, Lady Crieff," he said. His head was indeed lowered humbly, but his bold lips were grinning. "I have it from all quarters that I behaved abominably last evening."

"So you did, sir," she replied, with a pert glance. "You called me a wench!"

"It was the brandy speaking. I place half the blame in your own dish. No lady has the right to be so deuced pretty."

"Take care, sir," she replied, peering at him from the corners of her eyes. "Flattery will get you nowhere."

"I do not wish to be anywhere—except at your feet."

She gave a careless laugh. "Run along, Mr. Ponsonby. Every dog has his bite. You are forgiven this time, but I shall expect you to behave yourself in future."

He lifted her hand and placed an ardent kiss on her fingers. "An angel—merciful as well as beautiful. Dare I push my luck further and ask if you will give me a dance this evening? You will come. Say you will."

"I shall be here. If you are sober, then you may have a dance."

"Not a drop of wine will pass these lips until we meet again. Your obedient servant, milady."

He performed a sweeping bow and headed straight to the small room, where he ordered a glass of ale, assuring himself that ale was not wine, and a man had to have a drink from time to time if he was not to die of thirst.

When Moira and Jonathon were alone, she said, "Word of Lady Crieff's fortune has got about somehow. I wonder if the whole is known. Hang about belowstairs after breakfast and see what you can discover."

As Jonathon would not be available to escort her for a walk that morning, Moira was in no hurry to leave the Great Room. After breakfast, she went to the settee to have a glance at some magazines placed on the table for the guests' convenience. She noticed that although Mr. Hartly was in the room, he had not come rushing forward like the others. Perhaps he had not learned how rich Lady Crieff was. As he had not so much as bowed in her direction, she assumed their drive was off. Her first sense of shame soon turned to anger. *He* was the one who had behaved so wretchedly! Why should she feel embarrassed? No matter—she had her own carriage if she wished to go out.

She began reading an article about the repressive measures Parliament was instituting since the attempt on the Prince Regent's life in January. Caught up in it, she did not notice when Mr. Hartly finished his breakfast and walked toward her.

"Lady Crieff," he said, with a civil bow. "As you see, my prayers were answered. The Lord is merciful, even to a sinner. The sun is shining."

"Is it?" she asked, peering to the yew-shrouded windows. "It is difficult to tell from inside. Oh! You mean you wish to go driving after all. I was not sure after last night. . . ."

Her cheeks felt warm at the memory of that catastrophic encounter. Her only consolation was that Mr. Hartly was also ill at ease. He was not quite blushing, but his manner revealed constraint.

"The less said about last night, the better, except to proffer my apologies. Unlike Mr. Ponsonby, I do not have the excuse of drunkenness. If you wish to cry off, I understand. If, on the other hand, you can find it in your kindness to forgive me, I promise there will be no repetition of my behavior on that other occasion."

Moira had now established a good contact with Lionel March and had no real need of Hartly. Even if those two were involved in some business, Stanby was still interested in her. She could afford to be stiff with Hartly. Yet she did not wish to alienate him either. Of the three gentlemen at the inn, he was the only one in whom she felt any personal interest.

He tilted his head to one side and ventured a small smile. "Every dog has his bite," he reminded her. "You forgave Ponsonby. We have all been eavesdropping shamelessly. Come now, you must not reward drunkenness and be severe on sobriety. The days are long and tedious here. Why enliven them with a grudge, when they can be more pleasantly passed with an outing—suitably accompanied by Sir David."

She smiled reluctantly. "You are right. And to set the seal on my propriety, I shall ask you to come with me this afternoon to pay a call on my cousin, Lady Marchbank." If he balked at that, then he was up to no good.

"I should enjoy meeting her. One hears Cove House is a remarkable piece of architecture."

"An old Gothic heap, my cousin calls it."

"Just so." He sat down beside her. "Gothic heaps are all the fashion again, since Walpole built his little place on Strawberry Hill."

"I have not heard about this place," she said. "It sounds an unlikely spot for a Gothic house. Strawberries have no menace."

"The worst they portend is a duke." She frowned at this seeming irrelevancy. "They are used on the door of a ducal carriage," he added. Odd a lady did not know it. "Perhaps the custom is not followed in Scotland." Lady Crieff had nothing to say to this.

He spoke on enthusiastically about Walpole's mansion. This led easily to a discussion of Gothic novels, since Walpole's *Castle of Otranto* had been written at Strawberry Hill, using his own house as a background. He soon learned Lady Crieff was knowledgeable about Gothic novels. Her girlish enthusiasm for black veils and secret doors suggested an immaturity he had not felt last night, nor did she fall into any outrageous vulgarity.

After half an hour, Hartly called for fresh coffee, and they settled in like friends.

"I see you have overcome your aversion to Major Stanby. I was eavesdropping when he accosted you at breakfast, too," he said shamelessly.

"He did seem very friendly."

"No sly looks from the green eyes?" he asked playfully.

"No, I believe he must have heard something about my history, for he was noticeably approving. He even asked me for a dance."

"It is remarkable how a fortune improves a lady's character," he said, and laughed.

"Oh!" She gave a *tsk* of annoyance. "I cannot imagine how anyone in this out-of-the-way place learned about me. You—you have heard, too, then?"

"It is as well known as an old ballad by now that you are the wealthy young widow of an elderly Scottish squire. I do not know how word got about. Perhaps the locals had it of Lady Marchbank."

"Very likely that is it." How clever of Cousin Marchbank!

"I still say old Stanby wants watching," he said, making a joke of it now. "He is not too old to stand up and jig it, as he told you himself."

"You do have big ears, Mr. Hartly!"

"I can hear a church bell ringing—and a warning bell. Take care or you will find yourself saddled with another older husband."

"One was enough!" she said with feeling. At Mr. Hartly's shocked expression, she feared she was overdoing the vulgarity. "Not that I mean Sir Aubrey was a bad husband. He was the soul of generosity. It is just that—" She stopped, searching her mind for some excuse for having disparaged him. "We were not well-off, you see. Papa was so pleased when he offered. And really, Aubrey was very kind. He was always good to me."

"A lady has no need to apologize for marrying well, Lady Crieff. It is no new thing under the sun. May and December do not jog along together. That, too, is old history. December should realize it if May does not."

Yet he was annoyed that Lady Crieff had married an old man for money. She was young, with a young woman's passion. With her beauty, she could have married a young and wealthy gentleman. It seemed obscene to think of her in the arms of a gouty old laird. But of course she had assumed this veneer of gentility, which still slipped upon occasion, when she married her husband. As it was none of his concern, he soon spoke of other things.

When David returned, she rose. "Will two o'clock be convenient for our drive, Mr. Hartly?" she asked.

"Fine. I look forward to it."

Moira and Jonathon went upstairs. As soon as they were beyond hearing, she said, "What are they saying about us in the taproom?"

"Ponsonby used the term cream-pot love. They think you married Crieff for his blunt."

"But do they know about the jewelry?" she asked.

"I believe so. They lowered their voices when I was nearby, but I heard Ponsonby say to Stanby, 'Where do you think she has them?' I am sure they were talking about the jewelry."

"Good! And it all happened without our saying a word. That is the best way."

Jonathon sat looking out the window, the picture of youthful restlessness. "I wish we had brought our mounts. P'raps Cousin Vera can lend us a pair of prads. It is damned tedious sitting about all day."

"You brought your Latin reader," she reminded him.

He groaned when she put the book in his hands and took up her embroidery to sit with him and make sure he worked. The morning passed in this quiet fashion.

At luncheon, Ponsonby flirted with Moira across the room, ostentatiously holding up his glass of water to toast her each time he caught her eye. The major stopped and gave her a box of sugarplums.

"A poor gift for a lady, but in this little village, they have not heard of such a thing as marchpane, or sugared cherries."

"You are too kind, Major," she said, accepting the token. Jonathon loved sugarplums.

Mr. Hartly had another bottle of wine sent to their table.

"We should have used this stunt before," Jonathon said. "I had no idea ladies and sirs got so many gifts."

"They are not gifts, David; they are bait."

"I thought you and the jewels were the bait."

"That is for our trap. March believes he is setting a trap of his own."

"And Hartly as well?" he asked, looking at the wine.

That brought a frown to her face. Mr. Hartly was an agreeable young gentleman. She was beginning to hope his interest was personal—though there was no getting around the fact that he had been inquiring for Major Stanby when he arrived at the inn.

"Perhaps. Time will tell."

Chapter Seven

The corkscrew curls had softened to gentle waves by afternoon. Moira arranged them en corbeil and wore the same elaborately feathered bonnet and green sarcenet mantle in which she had arrived at Owl House Inn the day before. She regretted the overly ornate plumage of the bonnet. She had a keen fashion sense and had enjoyed accumulating her wardrobe. Schooled to practicality, she meant to wear the garments after her role of Lady Crieff was terminated, so the clothing was to her own taste, embellished to vulgarity by gewgaws that could be removed later. The sarcenet mantle was trimmed in gold satin and brass buttons. Excitement lent a sparkle to her eyes and a spring to her step.

Jonathon carried a large wicker basket, bearing an embroidered tablecloth worked by Moira's own hands for Lady Marchbank. She had been kind to the Trevithicks during their difficult period. Small presents of cash were only a part of it; she had provided moral support, and an offer that both Moira and Jonathon were welcome to make their home at Cove House if worst came to worst and they lost the Elms.

Mr. Hartly met them in the lobby. He was no expert on ladies' toilettes and felt he was out-of-date besides after his stint in Spain, but he knew instinctively that Moira would look prettier without that tower of feathers atop her head. He came forward to greet the youngsters.

"You will have to give me directions to Cove House," he said, after greeting them.

"Cousin Vera sent us a map. Here it is," Jonathon said, handing him a hand-drawn map. "P'raps you ought to give it to your groom."

They went outside, where a shining black carriage and bang-up team of bays awaited them.

"I say! That's something like!" Jonathon exclaimed. "Can I sit on the box with John Groom, Mr. Hartly?"

"You will get covered in dust, David," his sister cautioned.

Hartly smiled at the lad's enthusiasm. "I keep my traveling coat in the carriage. I like to take the reins myself from time to time. You are welcome to wear it, Sir David, if Lady Crieff—"

"Oh, very well," Moira agreed, although she would have preferred that Jonathon accompany her inside the carriage, to ease what might be a trying trip.

The coat fit as to length. Jonathon placed the basket on the floor of the carriage and leapt up on the perch with John Groom. Hartly was curious about that basket. Did it, by any chance, contain the Crieff jewelry collection? If so, it was an excellent idea to leave it with the Marchbanks, now that word of its existence had got about the inn.

As they drove along, Moira noticed that Hartly's eyes strayed to the basket from time to time.

"A little gift for my cousin Vera," she mentioned. "I made it myself. You will see it when we arrive—if you are interested in embroidery. I dare-say you are not. It took me months to make it."

"Is that how you passed your time in Scotland, Lady Crieff, with needlework?"

"Needlework and Gothic novels. I am a sad, shatter-brained creature," she replied.

Yet he remembered very well she had been reading a complex article on politics when he interrupted her that morning, and reading it with considerable interest. Her healthy face and lithe body told him she did not spend her entire day warming a sofa. Other than the clothes, she seemed like a genteel provincial, excited by even a simple call on a relative. At times, he felt there were two Lady Crieffs—one a wanton, the other a lady he could easily grow fond of.

She looked out at the passing scenery. "This is horrid countryside, is it not?" she asked. "All those flat marshes, so unlike the lush and rolling hills of—of Scotland," she said, pulling herself up short.

He noticed her hesitation and wondered at it. No doubt Scotland had lush and rolling hills, but it was more famous for its rocky Highlands. Surely sheep were raised on those rocky bluffs. Lush and rolling hills were more suitable to cattle.

"Take away the water and we could be in parts of Devon," he replied blandly. "The moors, you know."

"I hear they are desolate and dangerous," she replied, making conversation.

"It is easy to lose your way, but they are not all desolation. There are villages tucked in along the road. My own estate is not on the moors. Parts of Devon are well cultivated and civilized."

Moira gazed dreamily out the window. "It is strange that a tiny island like Britain has such varied landscapes, is it not? Everything from this"—she gestured to the view beyond the window—"to the Highlands, to the chalk downs, to the beautiful Lake District and London. All we lack is a desert, and we would be a world unto ourselves."

This seemed a rather serious thought for the hoyden Lady Crieff had acted last night. It confirmed his view that the girl was an anomaly. The face of a provincial miss, wearing a lightskirt's bonnet. He made a noncommittal reply.

Moira found the conversational going extremely rough. Not only was she worried that Hartly would make physical advances, she also had to remember to be vulgar, yet not so vulgar as to disgust him, if it turned out he was not a friend of Stanby's.

"You have an excellent team" was her next effort. "David will be enjoying himself immensely."

"He seems a nice lad. Does he give you much trouble?"

"David, trouble? Good Lord, no. I don't know what I should do without him." Now, why was he frowning like that?

"You will soon find out," he said. "He is returning to Penworth when you remove to London, is he not?"

"Indeed he is, but I shall have other company once I reach London. I know people there. He has provided good company on a long evening," she added.

It was a relief when the spires of Cove House appeared before them, soaring into the misty sky. The house was indeed a Gothic heap, complete with moldy stone, pointed windows, and even a pair of flying buttresses. The land around it was so damp and low-lying that it created a sort of moat, unfortunately without a drawbridge. The road had been raised to allow carriages to enter. Hartly thought it a derelict old place, but when he glanced at Lady Crieff, he saw her face was dazed with ecstasy.

"Oh, if I had known it was this lovely, I would have come when Cousin Vera invited us to live here!" she exclaimed.

A quick frown creased Hartly's brow. He had assumed Lady Marchbank was some kin to the Crieffs. Why would she invite Lady Crieff and David to live with her when David had Penworth Hall?

"After your husband's death, do you mean?" he asked.

For a fleeting moment, she stared at him, startled. "Yes, that was my meaning."

"She wanted you and David to live with her?"

"Yes. David was younger then, of course, as I was myself. David has an uncle who is his legal guardian. He would have managed Penworth. Cousin Vera thought we might like a holiday away from home. I did not mean 'live' in the sense of move here permanently."

"I see." Yet she had said "live here," in no uncertain terms.

Moira was glad when the carriage rattled to a stop and the groom hopped down to open the door. Jonathon was right behind him.

"By Jove, that was something like! Cooper let me take the reins—he held on, too, but I was driving."

"Best take off Mr. Hartly's coat before we go in," Moira said.

Jonathon did so and picked up the basket. It was clear Lady Marchbank had been awaiting their arrival, for she was at the door herself to greet them. Moira searched her mind in vain for a memory of this relative. She knew Lady Marchbank had visited her parents fifteen years earlier, but there had been many relatives visiting in those days. She was looking at a stranger: a tall, raw-boned elderly lady wearing an old-fashioned lace cap with lappets hanging over her ears. She had a large nose, not unlike Jonathon's, but it seemed more prominent on a lady. Her gray eyes were moist with tears.

She threw her arms around Moira and kissed her on both cheeks. "A beauty! You have grown into a beauty! I knew it would be so when I first laid eyes on you a decade and a half ago." She turned to Jonathon. "And this is little David," she said, with a sly eye at Moira, as if to say, "See, I remembered not to call him Jon." Then she turned to Hartly. "Now this lad I do not remember. Is he your cousin Jeremy, Bonnie?" The journals had not given Lady Crieff's first name. They had selected Bonnie as appropriately Scottish.

"This is Mr. Hartly, a gentleman who is staying at the inn and has given us a drive here," Moira explained hastily. She should have sent Cousin Vera a note to alert her to this change of plans.

Hartly bowed.

"So kind of you," Lady Marchbank said to him. "But why are we standing on the doorstep? Come in, come in. I have had Crook prepare us a dandy tea. How is that for a name, eh? My cook is called Crook. I always call her Crook. She hates it." On this ill-natured speech she emitted a tinny laugh.

They were led into a dim hallway that belonged in one of Mrs. Radcliffe's Gothic novels. A dark stairway curved sinuously at one end, to disappear in shadows. Antique portraits in aged frames glowered at them from the walls. A stuffed eagle was perched on a pedestal, wings spread, as if he were about to attack. His glass eyes glittered menacingly.

"I say! Look at that, Lady Crieff!" Jonathon exclaimed. "Do you have a dungeon with chains and bones, Cousin Vera?"

"No, but we have a secret passage to the caves below. My husband's ancestors made their fortune smuggling wool in the old days. Oh, we are a wicked crew here, wicked!" She cackled like a witch.

Lady Marchbank led them into the main saloon, another tenebrous chamber with creaking Jacobean paneling and faded window hangings.

"There is no point trying to be stylish here," she told them. "Between the damp sea air and the smoke from the grate, everything is destroyed. I had those window hangings put up only three years ago. Or was it five? No matter, they cost me a small fortune and looked like rags within a twelvemonth."

She bundled them onto a pair of sofas before the grate, where a few logs burned desultorily. "Danby! Danby, I say. I want my tea!" she hollered into the depths of the hallway beyond.

An aged butler appeared at the doorway. "Just coming, your ladyship," he said, and vanished into the gloom.

"I have brought you the tablecloth I wrote about, cousin," Moira said, handing Lady Marchbank the basket.

Lady Marchbank opened it with age-speckled hands. The knuckles were swollen, but she could move her fingers quite well. She drew out a large linen tablecloth, worked around the edges and down the center with intertwining vines and flowers in pale shades of green and gold.

"Oh, Bonnie! You shouldn't have! This is gorgeous. Much too fine for an old lady like me. We never entertain anyone who deserves this. I shall put it on my bed for a coverlet. That is what I shall do. If I put it on the table, John would only spill his brandy on it."

"I am glad you like it. Where is Cousin John?" Moira asked.

"Out and about somewhere. He will be back in time to meet you."

Hartly remembered that the excuse for not putting up with the Marchbanks was Lord Marchbank's ailing health, yet he was well enough to be up and about. Another small mystery. He was surprised to see that the wicker basket did not hold a padlocked case. He took a surreptitious peek into it while the ladies examined the tablecloth. The cloth had not filled the basket. There were newspapers folded up below it, obviously with something else beneath.

"We brought some preserves as well," Moira mentioned. "The marmalade you like so much."

Lady Marchbank continued examining the cloth. "Such a lot of work. I don't know how you found time to do it, so busy as you must have been."

Moira knew the old lady was thinking of her real

life—trying to make ends meet on the estate—and spoke up quickly to remind her of her role.

"I had a deal of help running Penworth Hall," she said.

"Of course you did, but a young gel likes to ride and entertain and that sort of thing."

The tea tray arrived, a veritable feast, with a pigeon pie, cold cuts, bread and three kinds of cheese, a plum cake, and various sweets. It was impossible to do justice to it so soon after lunch.

After they had eaten, Hartly said, "I shall go out and have a walk along the beach while you cousins catch up on all the family gossip."

"I shall go with you," Jonathon added. "I saw a nifty ship through the window. It looked as if it was coming into your dock, Cousin Vera."

The lady gave him a sharp look. "That would be Homer Guthrie's fishing smack. He stops here to let us choose what we want from his catch. I would not bother him if I were you, David. He is a testy old fellow. Why do you not take Mr. Hartly to see the stables? No, on second thought, that is not a good idea. One of the colts has been gelded and is in a bad mood. . . . I have it! Take Mr. Hartly along the west cliff. You will get a pretty view of the cove there. Turn left when you go out the front door."

After they left, Lady Marchbank turned a laughing face to her remaining guest. "Gracious! I almost wish they were not going out, but then we could not talk in front of Hartly. John runs the smuggling hereabouts, you must know. Guthrie is bringing in a load now."

"Really! You mean Cousin John is the Black Ghost?"

"Good gracious, no. He is well past that sort of

flying about at night. The Black Ghost is merely a goblin to frighten the simple village folks. It is John's nephew, Peter Masters, from Romney. He runs the operation there. He will take over the Blaxstead run as well when John retires. John has a cozy setup here, as he is the magistrate. No harm in it, eh?"

"It seems to be accepted by everyone except the government," Moira conceded.

"It is all that keeps body and soul together for the local families. Of course, I would not like you to tell Hartly any of this. He might very well be a Revenueman sent down from London. They pull off those sly tricks from time to time."

"Oh, dear! Do you think that possible?" Moira exclaimed.

"There is no saying. Did you plan to make him your beau? I take it he does not know who you really are."

"He has no idea. He is just a man staying at the inn. He was asking for Major Stanby, which is why I am a little interested in him."

She gave a cagey smile. "He is monstrously handsome. An ex-officer, I take it?"

"Why, no, he said he has an estate in Devon."

"He walks like a soldier, and he has the swarthy complexion of the fellows returned from Spain. Returned officers have been given these plum jobs with the Revenue Service before. Keep an eye on him for us. John will want to know what he is up to. But if he was asking for Stanby, perhaps he is with Bow Street. The police must be onto the bounder by now."

"I had not thought of that!"

"Do not trust him until you learn for certain. Perhaps he is what they call a Corinthian, a sportsman, just having a holiday by the sea. Some of them turn a wretched tan color from being outdoors. Now, tell me all about your adventure. Have you hooked old Lionel March, the bounder?"

"I have scraped an acquaintance. In fact, I shall be standing up with him at an assembly at the inn this evening."

"Excellent! I shall be there. My presence will confirm that you are indeed Lady Crieff. Between us, we'll reel him in and gaff him. I think, Moira, that you ought to wear some real jewelry this evening."

"I have been wearing my diamond necklace."

"That is good, but to keep wearing one piece when you have a whole collection—it does not seem natural. I slipped the word to our junior footman that Lady Crieff is rich as a nabob and has a fabulous collection of jewelry. His sister works for Mrs. Abercrombie in Blaxstead, so the word will be out by now. I shall show you my jewelry, and you shall tell me if any of it matches items in the Crieff collection."

She led Moira to her bedroom, another large, ugly room, and took out a wooden box that she kept hidden in a hatbox. Her jewels were antiquated and were not a good match for the Crieff collection. There was one set of sapphires that might pass inspection.

"My ball gown is green," Moira said. "I could not wear sapphires with it."

"But they are not so valuable as emeralds or diamonds. That might provide an excuse for wearing them at a public inn."

"I would be nervous having them at the inn, cousin."

"I shall take them home with me after the rout. How is that?"

"That should be safe enough," Moira said.

She put the sapphires in her handkerchief in the bottom of her reticule and they returned belowstairs.

They refilled their teacups and settled in for a good cose.

Outside, Hartly did not turn left. He headed straight for the beach and the fishing smack. He had already observed that Cove House was ideally situated for smuggling. The ship at the dock was similar to the one that had stopped at Owl House to unload brandy, concealed beneath its cargo of mackerel. Lady Marchbank's feeble excuse for keeping them away from the stable suggested that the cargo was being transferred there. The only impediment to confirming this was David. He had to get rid of the lad, preferably in a manner that would not raise his suspicions.

"You did not think to ask your cousin about that cave," he said. "That would be something to see. I daresay it would not be the thing to interrupt the ladies' cose. Pity."

Jonathon stopped in his tracks. "You go on ahead, Mr. Hartly. I shall meet up with you later. I just remembered something I have to tell Cousin Vera. She wanted to know about . . . about what school I shall be going to next autumn."

He scooted off, leaving Hartly with another question. He had assumed Sir David was being educated at home with a tutor. But if so, why change the routine at this time, when his presence at Penworth would be useful? He was reaching the age when he should be learning about the management of his estate, especially with his papa dead.

A few other items bothered him as well. Lady Marchbank's reference to seeing Lady Crieff when she was a child suggested the relationship was with the girl's family, not Sir Aubrey's. It seemed unlikely that a simple shepherd from Scotland was related to Lady Marchbank. He wondered, too, what else the wicker basket contained besides the tablecloth.

These were matters he might best discover by watching and listening later. For the present, he wished to confirm that Cove House was being used for smuggling. Some highly placed people were involved, Bullion had said. Who, in the area, was more highly placed than Lord Marchbank? Was it possible old Marchbank was the infamous Black Ghost? Hartly meant to be back at Cove House in time to meet him.

He approached the fishing ship cautiously, crouching behind rocks. An elderly gentleman was there, giving orders. He was indeed selecting a few fish, but e'er long, he looked all about, then said something to the man in charge of the ship. Half a dozen fishermen were called, and there, in broad daylight, twenty-four barrels were rolled ashore. A youngster soon appeared, leading two donkeys. A pair of barrels was put over the animals' backs, one on either side, and the donkeys were led off, presumably to either the stable or the cave, where they would be concealed until picked up for further shipment.

Hartly had seen enough. He began walking along to the west, as Lady Marchbank had suggested. The donkeys were heading east, toward the stable. After half an hour, David had not joined him, so he returned to the saloon.

"Where is David?" Moira asked at once.

Hartly had forgotten all about him. "Did he not return here? He said he wished to tell Lady Marchbank something."

Moira felt cold fingers tapping at her spine. Hartly had kidnapped Jonathon! Right under their noses, he had spirited him away.

She leapt to her feet. "What have you done with him?" she gasped.

Hartly's stunned face told her she had guessed wrong. Before he could reply, Jonathon came prancing in, covered with dust and cobwebs.

"I say, Cousin Vera! That secret passage is something like!"

Moira collapsed in relief onto the sofa. It was Lady Marchbank who had turned a ghastly shade of gray.

"How did you find it?" she demanded. Her eyes slewed accusingly to Mr. Hartly, who was gazing unconcernedly out the window.

Jonathon said, "Why, I just opened that little blue door at the side of the house, and there it was. Why do you keep so many bar—"

"You should not have been snooping without permission, David," she scolded. "There are rats down there. You might have been bitten and caught the plague. It is a nasty, dirty place. Now come and apologize. There's a good lad."

The little incident was smoothed over, but after such displays of temper, the mood was uncertain. They all heard the heavy footsteps sounding in the hallway. Lady Marchbank announced, "Ah, here is John, at last," with a great air of relief, as if he were Christopher Columbus, safely returned from his journey to the New World.

Chapter Eight

Hartly knew at a glance that the obese, gouty old gentleman hobbling into the room was not the Black Ghost, but he was the same gentleman who had overseen the unloading of the brandy at the cove earlier. Lord Marchbank had imbibed too much of the cargo that landed at his doorstep to take such an active part in the smuggling. His bulbous, veined nose and bloodshot eyes spoke of a long career of drinking. Brandy had not destroyed the man's mind, however. He gave Hartly one short, sharp look, then turned to welcome his cousins.

He did not remain in the saloon long, but his welcome was warm. He assured Sir David and Lady Crieff that they had only to send a note to Cove House if they required anything.

Lady Marchbank showed him the tablecloth, which he praised in the vague, hearty manner of one who did not appreciate what he saw but wished to compliment the giver.

"David mentioned he misses his rides, dear," Lady Marchbank said. "I have told Bonnie she may ride my mount while she is here. Have you anything in the stable that would do for David?"

"Come along and take your pick, lad," Marchbank offered at once. Almost immediately, he changed the offer. "On t'other hand, I shall have my groom send a mount around with the carriage when you leave. The nags are restless this afternoon. Gray Lady is foaling. It always upsets the animals."

"And as I mentioned to the children earlier," his wife added, "that bay colt has been gelded, and he is upset, too."

"Aye, the stables are a regular hospital," Marchbank said. His plummy cheeks had turned a shade deeper, confirming Hartly's suspicion that the stables were no horse hospital but a holding den for that cargo brought in that afternoon in broad daylight. When Marchbank reached for the brandy bottle on a side table, his wife caught his eye and shook her head in warning. Marchbank poured himself a glass of wine instead.

After a little discussion of a mount for David, the guests rose to leave.

"I shall arrive at the inn at eight, to chaperon you for the assembly," Lady Marchbank told Moira.

"Will you also come, sir?" Moira asked Marchbank.

"John will not come," Lady Marchbank answered for him. "He detests parties of all things. If I waited for him to take me out, I should never see the light of day."

The guests were accompanied to the door. Marchbank went out to the carriage with them.

While Jonathon and Moira examined their mounts, Marchbank had a private word with Hartly.

"Finding Blaxstead a trifle dull, I daresay?" he mentioned.

"On the contrary, sir, I find it full of interesting activity. Mind you, I am thinking of changing inns. I had a small sum stolen from my room last night. I have made no formal complaint, but I have reason to believe it was one of the young fellows who work for Bullion. Who is the magistrate hereabouts?"

"You are looking at him. Gather up your evidence and we'll toss him into jail. That sort of petty pilfering gives the village a bad name."

"It was a small sum. As I am remaining only a few days, perhaps it is not worth my while. I shan't leave money in my room another time."

"That might be best. Tip Bullion the clue as well. He will not want a thief working for him."

Jonathon called Hartly to go and see his mount, and that terminated the short conversation. Soon the guests took their departure.

Moira was quiet on the way home. She had a good deal to think about. If Hartly was here to spy on the smugglers, then he was not working with Stanby. There had been a card game last night, which tended to confirm Jonathon's notion that it was only the hope of such a game that had made Hartly ask for Stanby. Hartly still posed a threat, but a threat of a different sort. He was out to put a stop to Marchbank's smuggling. She would keep an eye on him, as Cousin Vera had asked.

She came to rigid attention when he said to Jonathon, "How were the caves? Were they interesting?"

"They were dark and wet and full of barrels," Jonathon replied.

Moira gave an involuntary jerk. This was as good as telling Hartly that Marchbank was a smuggler. "Cousin Vera told me she keeps her pickle barrels down there," she said.

"She must make an awful lot of pickles," Jonathon said. He received such a gimlet stare from his sister that he realized he was being indiscreet. "Now that you mention it, there was a smell of vinegar in the cave. There were not that many barrels, actually."

"You know how Lord Marchbank loves his pickles," she said.

Hartly's laughing eye told her she had not fooled him for a minute. He knew she had not seen her cousins since she was a child. How should she know he loved pickles? There had been no pickles served at tea.

"Are you sure it was not brandied fruit that was kept there? Or just brandy, without the fruit," he said playfully.

"My cousin would never tolerate such a thing!" she said.

"Perhaps the smugglers are using his caves—without his knowledge, of course," Hartly suggested.

She leapt on it like a cat on catnip. "Very likely that is it. I shall warn Lord Marchbank. He will want to put a guard in the caves to catch the Gentlemen."

"The locals will not thank him for it," Hartly said. "I should think half the population make their living from smuggling."

She was not conned by this pretended approval,

designed to lure her into revealing family secrets. "Surely not. My cousin would never countenance such a thing."

"He countenances a bottle of brandy in his saloon. I was hoping he would offer me a tipple."

"Very likely it is kept for medicinal purposes. Marchbank suffers from gout."

"I rather think what he is using for a cure is the cause of his affliction."

Jonathon came to the rescue by changing the subject. "I think we ought to change mounts, Lady Crieff," he said. "The mare Cousin Vera lent you is bigger than my gelding."

"Marchbank said Firefly was a lively goer. I am using Cousin Vera's mare. The saddle is a lady's saddle."

"I daresay we could change saddles."

"No, you said yourself Firefly is smaller."

Hartly did not try to reintroduce the subject of smuggling, but he had noticed how eager Lady Crieff was to drop it.

Jonathon wanted to give Firefly a try as soon as they arrived back at Owl House. With an assembly to prepare for, Moira decided to wait until the next morning. She had to prepare her own toilette.

Hartly went to his room for a word with Mott. He found his "valet" stretched out on his bed, reading the racing news.

"What has Stanby been up to?" he asked.

"A damned funny thing," Mott replied. "He was at Lady Crieff's room, stuffing a note under her door. I tried to get it out with a knife, but it was in too far. Do you think they are partners?"

"No, I rather think he has decided to make a try for her jewelry."

"Did you learn anything at the Marchbanks'?"

"Yes. Marchbank is working hand in glove with the Black Ghost. He allows the smugglers to use his place. A cargo was being unloaded while I was there. He has the caves under his house full of brandy. From there, it goes to his stable, for eventual shipment about the countryside. As he is the magistrate, he would see that none of the men are convicted. Bullion mentioned people in higher places, you recall."

"Is it possible Marchbank is the Black Ghost?"

"Black elephant would be more like it. He is fat as a flawn, full of gout, and slow-moving. I doubt an elderly lord would put himself to so much bother and danger."

"What do you plan to do about it?" Mott asked.

"As our card game this evening has been canceled for the assembly, I think I shall go ahead with the smuggling business. We could not hope to get fifteen thousand in one sitting at cards in any case, and we both want to finish the business as quickly as possible. I fancy Stanby will make a try for Lady Crieff's jewelry. If he gets hold of it, he will be gone in short order. I wonder what that note to Lady Crieff said."

"I tried to get into her room, but I had no luck."

"What was Ponsonby up to?"

"He and Stanby were out driving together. I would give a monkey to know what Ponsonby's game is. Do you think Stanby imported him to use as a dupe during future card games?"

"Stanby has always worked alone in the past."

"Ponsonby tries to give the impression he is from the very tip of the ton. He cannot speak without dropping a title. There was no mention in the journals of any duel in London recently. You recall that killing Noddy was his excuse for being here."

Hartly poured himself a glass of wine and went to the window, where he looked out at the estuary. "Stanby, Lady Crieff, and Ponsonby. Is it possible Ponsonby and Lady Crieff are working together, trying to peddle paste jewels? That would account for his dropping of titled names, to give an illusion of wealth and prestige."

"And they have selected Stanby as their victim, you mean?"

"Yes, most unwisely. They'll not put anything over on that wily customer. He will require a more likely investment than paste jewels. Now that I know how the smuggling hereabouts is handled, I think I can convince him to invest. We shall need a good reason for the Black Ghost to be retiring from such a profitable venture. Now, what local worthy shall we pretend is the Black Ghost?"

"Why not Marchbank? He is elderly, I think you said?"

"Not young, and with that gout . . . Yes, I think he might very well be ready to sell out—for a stiff price. We will need yet another Black Ghost to introduce to Stanby."

The men exchanged a laughing look.

"They don't come much blacker than your batman," Mott said.

"I shall send a message to London asking Gibbs to procure a black hat, domino, and mount and come at once. He was angry with me for not letting him come. He cannot put up here, but he must be close by. Snargate will do. I shall write to him now. And you, Mott, will call for hot water. It is time to give your master a shave. I must be in face for the assembly this evening."

"I shall ring for the water. I dare not show my worthless hide belowstairs. The malkin, Maggie, has forbidden me to darken the door of her kitchen—thank God."

Mott rang, and when the servant girl came, he wore his petulant face and used his fluting voice.

"Hot water, mind, not lukewarm, as you sent up this morning. And remind Cook about the bread sauce."

"Forget the bread sauce," Hartly said.

Mott pouted. "But you adore my bread sauce!"

The servant giggled and left.

In her room, Moira espied the paper on the floor and picked it up, frowning. She opened it and read, "My Dear Lady Crieff: I pray you will forgive my interference on a matter that is none of my business. My only excuse is my greater years and experience, and concern for your position. It is widely bruited about the inn that you are traveling with a valuable collection of jewelry. With such unknown parties as a certain p*** staying here, I fear for their—and your—safety. I have undertaken to remove p*** from the inn during your absence. I strongly recommend that you put your jewels in a safe place. Bullion is boasting that they are in his safe. Perhaps your cousin, Lady Marchbank, would keep them for you? Once again, please forgive my interfering. I have only your welfare at heart. I look forward to the pleasure of standing up with you this evening. Yr. faithful servant, Stanby."

Moira sniffed and tossed the note aside. She saw through Stanby's stunt. He was putting himself forward as her protector. She could not fathom, as yet, how he planned to end up with the jewels, but she knew as surely as she knew her name that that was his aim.

The note suggested that he had fallen for the story, at least, and that was a good step forward.

Chapter Nine

The guests collected in the Great Room for dinner that evening were en grande toilette, with manners to match. Bows and curtseys assumed an elegance seldom seen at Owl House. Ponsonby had rigged himself out in a burgundy velvet jacket that set off his burnished curls to great advantage. He scraped a leg, simpered, and lifted the inevitable glass of water in Lady Crieff's direction when she entered the room. Major Stanby went forward to greet her. He wore a sedate black jacket, with a fine diamond in his cravat.

"You had my note?" he asked in a conspiratorial voice.

"Indeed I did, Major. I thank you for your concern." Her instinct, when she was with him, was always to get away as quickly as possible. This was too good an opening to miss, however, so she braced herself to do what was necessary. "It is a great worry, traveling with my jewelry. I am taking it to

London to sell, you see, else I would have left it at Cove House, as you mentioned."

"It would be safest if you could proceed to London at once."

"Ah, well, there are some—problems," she said, with a frowning pout. Then she turned to Jonathon. "Run along, David, and order us a bottle of champagne. We shall have champagne tonight for a special treat."

Jonathon left, and she inclined her head toward Stanby in a secretive way. "The fact is, Sir Aubrey's lawyers are being quite horrid," she told him. "The jewelry is the only thing he left me in his will, for Penworth, of course, is entailed on Sir David. Now the lawyers are trying to say my husband did not want me to have my own jewels, if you please! I thought it best to take them and run while I had the chance. I brought Sir David along to keep them from influencing him. He is so young and a regular greenhead. Sir David is in total agreement with me. He wants me to have the jewelry, but the lawyers say he cannot give it to me formally until he is one and twenty. He is only sixteen years old. How am I expected to live in the meanwhile? I do not want to stay at Penworth, with all the old cats squinting at me every time I step out."

"And you plan to sell the jewelry in London?" he asked, cutting through the rodomontade to the gist of the matter.

"Yes. I have an agent from a jewelry firm coming here to meet me. I thought the lawyers might have been in touch with the larger firms, like Love and Wirgams and Rundell and Bridges, so I have a man from a smaller company coming. I do not plan to go to London until I have my money in my pocket.

Once the collection is sold, the lawyers can hardly reclaim it, eh?" She allowed a cunning smile to alight on her lips.

"I see," Stanby said, nodding his approval. "An excellent notion, but you realize the jeweler will not give you a fair price when he sees your position."

"I am prepared for that," she said. "I know I shall lose half their worth, but as that will still leave me with fifty thousand, I can manage. I am not greedy."

"When do you expect this jeweler to arrive?"

"I was to write him when I reached Blaxstead. It was he who suggested meeting at this place."

Stanby saw a situation much to his liking. A hussy was running off with stolen valuables worth a fortune. She was exceedingly careless of both their safety and her own, to say nothing of the law. His eyes slid to the sapphires at her throat and ears. Worth a small fortune! If the rest of the stuff was of this quality . . . She was ready to take half of what the jewelry was worth—and with a little pressure, she might very well take half of half. Another possibility was simply to steal the jewels and make a run for it. Yet another idea was beginning to find approval. Lady Crieff was a pretty hussy. He had not had a "wife" for a few years. It might be amusing. . . .

"We shall speak of this again," he said, as people were beginning to look at them.

"Oh, yes, I do appreciate your interest, Major." Her eyelashes fluttered shamelessly. "I have always felt so safe with older gentlemen. Not that you are as old as Sir Aubrey. Indeed, you are hardly old at all. It is just that I am so young and foolish."

When she joined Jonathon at the table, she was trembling but happy. The major had behaved exactly as she had foreseen. His eyes fairly glowed with greed. A few heads turned to admire the young widow as she passed, Hartly's among them. He wondered at that tête-à-tête by the doorway. If Lady Crieff and Stanby were working together, he would not be so chummy with her in public, and it was he who had intercepted her, not vice versa.

She was looking particularly lovely this evening. A deep green gown of lutestring provided a dramatic contrast to her ivory skin. It shone in the lamplight, highlighting the lithe body beneath it. The gown was, unfortunately, somewhat overembellished with gold ribbons. The coiffure, as well, was too ornate for a young lady. Those whirls were seen on no one but lightskirts in London, but it would take more than a bad coiffure to destroy that face. The sapphires were not the optimum choice of jewels to wear with a green gown. He had heard that the Crieff collection included emeralds—why did she not wear them? Or diamonds. Diamonds were the champagne of jewelry; they went with anything.

He bowed when she passed his table. She stopped for a word, and Hartly rose.

"We will not be making depredations on your excellent wine this evening, Mr. Hartly. I am allowing Sir David to order champagne, in honor of the assembly. I am looking forward to it—the assembly, I mean."

"As I am, madam. I daresay Stanby has beaten me to the first dance?"

"No, we were speaking of something else." She allowed her fingers to play with the sapphires, to indicate in a seemingly unconscious way what they had been discussing. "Shall I give you the first dance?"

"I would be honored."

"It is settled, then. How horrid of me to interrupt your dinner. There is nothing so unappetizing as cold mutton. Do sit down, Mr. Hartly."

She waved and moved along, nodding to Ponsonby on the way.

"Am I allowed to have just one glass of wine with dinner?" he asked playfully.

"You shall have a glass of my champagne as a reward for being a good lad," she replied in the same spirit, and called Wilf to fill a glass for Mr. Ponsonby.

It was only a small assembly at a village inn, but still Moira felt the evening held the promise of some pleasure. The champagne lent a festive atmosphere, and the gentlemen were all done up in their best jackets. Mr. Hartly was the only one with any real claim to looks, of course. She would flirt with him and see if he let anything slip about his being a Revenueman.

Jonathon carried the burden of conversation at dinner. He waxed enthusiastic about Firefly and told Moira he had found a suitable ride for them to take the next morning.

"There is a church big enough to hold a couple of thousand people," he said, "which is strange, for there aren't above three dozen houses in the whole village. I daresay Blaxstead must have been a larger place once. I wonder what happened to all the people?"

"I have no idea," she said distractedly. Her mind

was working on how she could get Stanby to offer to buy the jewels.

When dinner was over, Bullion began to harry the servants into clearing the room of tables and chairs for the assembly. The gentlemen removed to the small room, but as there was a liberal sprinkling of undesirables there, Moira elected to await Cousin Vera in her room abovestairs. Jonathon remained below to watch and listen.

Lady Marchbank arrived shortly after eight.

"Have you learned anything about Hartly?" was her first question. "John is worried to death about him. I feared Jonathon might have mentioned all the barrels in the caves. That is where John stores his spare cargo."

"Jonathon did mention it, but Hartly suggested that the smugglers were using the caves without your knowledge."

"Ah, that is good! That is what we shall say if he asks. John disliked to remove them, for the cave is so handy. I shall tell him Hartly is onto that hiding place. The stream would be safer. Did Hartly do anything about the lad who stole money from him here at the inn?"

"What are you talking about, cousin?"

"He did not tell you someone took money from his room?"

"I heard nothing of it."

"Then John is right," she said grimly. "He made the story up on the spot. It was a ruse to confirm that John is the magistrate. We could be in a dreadful pickle if Hartly takes that tale to London. When anyone lays a charge against the Gentlemen, John always dismisses it for lack of evidence—after he has disposed of the evidence, of course. I fear

Hartly is working with the Customs people. Dear me, how can we get rid of him? Do you think he might be susceptible to a bribe?"

"That would only make your position worse, if he refused the bribe," Moira said.

"So it would. You could always marry him" was her next notion. "He would not report his own family. He is really quite handsome and gentlemanlike. Not in the style of your usual Preventive man."

"Marriage is a little drastic—and besides, he has not asked me. Jonathon and I shall watch him closely, cousin, and if he appears to be looking for evidence, we shall get word to you at once."

"There is a good lass. Bullion is keeping an eye peeled for us as well. Now, shall we go below? I feel like a jig tonight, but with my bad knees, I shall have to make do with a game of whist by the grate."

The Great Room had been cleared of all but two of its tables. They were set up near the grate for the older guests to play cards. A small platform had been brought in to hold the three musicians. The inn did not boast a pianoforte, but two fiddlers and one man with a cello were tuning their instruments. The limited space available and the small smattering of guests were only sufficient to make up four squares, three of them composed of the local gentry. Moira took her place with Hartly for the quadrille, Jonathon stood up with a local belle, and Ponsonby and Stanby found partners to complete the square.

Hartly paid a trite compliment to Moira on her appearance. Soon he moved on to more interesting matters. "It is a pity Lord Marchbank did not come to the assembly," he said. "He seemed well enough this afternoon."

"The gout comes and goes. He must have had an attack," she replied. She wondered if Marchbank was even then engaged in his illicit business, and if Hartly was prying to discover it.

She noticed that Hartly was examining her sapphires. "I daresay I should not wear my jewels at a public place like this, but if one does not wear them to parties, what good are they? Of course, I would not wear the Crieff emeralds to a place like this. They are much too valuable."

"It might be wise to leave them with the Marchbanks while you are at the inn," he suggested.

"That is odd! Major Stanby gave me exactly the same advice."

"Did he indeed!" Hartly was surprised to hear it. If Stanby meant to steal them, it would be more easily done from the inn. Was it possible the old goat had something different in mind . . . like offering for Lady Crieff?

"You and the major are becoming fast friends, I see."

"He is quite a father to me."

"I doubt if that is the relationship he has in mind. But of course Lady Crieff needs no advice on how to handle amorous gentlemen," he said, with a deprecating smile.

"Amorous! It is not that sort of friendship, I assure you. He is old as the hills," she said lightly, without a thought to her alleged old husband, Sir Aubrey.

Hartly smiled blandly. "Then may I consider

Stanby is not among the competition?" he asked boldly. "That leaves only Ponsonby and myself."

"Stiff competition for you indeed!" she replied, with a laughing sideways glance from her silver eyes.

"I enjoy a fair competition, but I trust you will not put me on a water diet, as you have Ponsonby."

"There is no need. You handle your wine like a proper gentleman. Then, too, if I forbid you to have wine at your table, you could not share it with me. I should be forced to drink Bullion's vinegar. Why does he serve such awful stuff, I wonder?"

"Because he is not accustomed to serving such out-and-outers as you and me, Lady Crieff, who can discern the difference."

"I am no connoisseur of wine, but I agree the clientele leaves something to be desired. Present company excepted—when he behaves himself."

"If that is a compliment, I thank you. You said the length of your stay was undecided, Lady Crieff. Have you come to any conclusion yet?"

"Why, Mr. Hartly, you sound as if you are trying to get rid of me."

"You would have to be shatter-brained to come to that conclusion—and you are not shatter-brained. My concern is that I must be off to London soon, and I wondered when I might expect to see you there. I should like to call on you, if you permit."

Moira's happiness at hearing he wished to continue the acquaintance was diluted with fear. Was he darting off to London to report to his superiors? "I have not decided when I shall go, nor where I shall stay. If you would give me your direction, I could let you know when I arrive."

"Alas, like yourself, I shall be putting up at whatever hotel has a room vacant. Is there no friend or relative I might apply to, to discover your address?"

"I have not decided whether I shall be in touch with Sir Aubrey's relatives or not. I have never met them. They might be horrid. It would be best if you gave me the name of someone I could notify when I arrive."

After a brief pause, Hartly said, "I shall be calling on my cousin, Lord Daniel Parrish, at Hanover Square. You could write to me there."

She blinked to hear him calmly drop a title into the conversation. Hartly must indeed be related to the gentleman, or he could not use his address. Lord Daniel might very well have got his cousin appointed to the plum position of Revenue inspector. It was beginning to seem that Cousin Vera was right, and Mr. Hartly was here at the behest of the government to snoop into smuggling. While this was vexing, it was better than having him allied with Stanby. She concluded that Hartly was a decent, respectable, handsome young gentleman—and he was receiving a wretched opinion of her.

A small, wistful sigh escaped her lips. Looking at her, Hartly was struck with her youth and unhappiness. He felt convinced that this innocent young girl had nothing to do with Stanby. She had been inveigled into marrying Sir Aubrey by an avaricious father, and now that her husband was dead, she was running off to London. There was nothing wrong in that. It was what any venturesome lady would do, if she had the pluck.

"I hope you will write to me at Hanover Square, Lady Crieff," he said earnestly. "I should like to see you again."

Upon hearing that note of earnestness, she

peered shyly at him. Their eyes held for a long moment, then the movements of the dance drew them apart. Moira felt she was really talking to Mr. Hartly for the first time. He seemed different tonight, more approachable. If he was here only because of smugglers, then she could tell him her true plight, and perhaps get him to help her.

What would he think of her, trying to steal twenty-five thousand pounds? Legally, that was what she was doing. The money was hers and Jonathon's by rights, but not by law. No, it was too risky to tell him, but perhaps, after she had regained her fortune, she might write to him at Hanover Square and see him again, away from Owl House. To confess a fait accompli was easier than to involve him in it.

"Yes, I shall write, Mr. Hartly," she said.

A look of gentle satisfaction settled on his face. "I consider that a promise. And by the by, my friends call me Daniel. It is a family name I share with Lord Daniel Parrish."

The old Lady Crieff would have smiled boldly and made some pert remark. This Lady Crieff blushed and said, "We have not been acquainted very long to be using first names, Mr. Hartly."

"That will teach me to try to force a friendship on an unwilling lady. My lesson last night was not enough for me."

"Oh, I am not unwilling! And last night was not entirely your fault. I . . . I should not have invited you in for wine. I have never been alone at an inn before—without a proper chaperon, I mean. One forgets there are not butlers or footmen about. I have been thinking about last night, and realize I should have been more careful. Using first names seems a little fast."

Her explanation satisfied Hartly's lingering doubts. A greenhead of a girl might very well be unaware of the danger in inviting a man into her room. Lady Crieff had not the advantage of a proper upbringing, but he felt her instincts were genteel.

"I look forward to calling you Bonnie, and hearing you call me Daniel, but we shall withhold first names until we meet again in London."

It was not until that moment that Moira realized she was, in fact, not going to London. She and Jonathon would return to the Elms, and she would never see Mr. Hartly again. It lent a bittersweet quality to the dance.

"When, exactly, are you leaving?" she asked, rather sadly.

He studied her for a moment, then said, "Do you know, I begin to think I shall prolong my stay a little."

"Oh, no! Please, you must not do so on my account." What had she done? He had been on the point of leaving, and she had induced him to remain, where he would create endless mischief for the Marchbanks, discovering even more details of the smuggling.

His eyebrows rose. "Well, now I am the one who feels you are trying to be rid of me."

"You must not change your plans on my account. I will not hear of it. Lord Daniel is expecting you."

"No, he is not. I shall call on him when I arrive, but he is not waiting on tenterhooks for me. I shall stay."

He wondered at her reaction—more resigned than happy.

Lady Crieff played the flirt with Stanby when she stood up with him. It was Stanby who had brought her to Blaxstead, and she was not about to lose sight of the fact, even though her mind kept harking back to Hartly.

Stanby said, "I have been thinking over what you told me, about selling your jewelry, Lady Crieff. Of course, it belongs to you by rights, but the law takes little account of rights."

"I know it well," she said grimly.

"If the pieces show up in London, they will be traced back to the jeweler, and eventually to you. Selling what does not legally belong to you is a hanging crime."

"But they are mine! I *must* sell them! I have not a sou to my name."

"My idea is that you place them with someone who could peddle them abroad for you."

"I need the money now. And how could I trust this 'someone'? I know no one who travels abroad."

"You know me," he said simply. "As to your needing money now, I could let you have—say, five thousand, in advance."

So that was his game, the sly rogue! "You are very kind, Major, and naturally I am not calling your character into question, but the fact is, I do not know you all that well."

He smiled benignly. "Time will remedy that, Lady Crieff. There is no immediate rush."

The major's arms felt like a serpent winding around her. Her flesh crawled, to see his gooseberry eyes alight with greed. She was vastly relieved when the dance was over.

Mr. Ponsonby claimed the next dance. He was a dead bore, but at least he was not Lionel March. Although Ponsonby had made a game of drinking water since yesterday, it was soon apparent that he had been consuming a deal of brandy or wine as well. Both his speech and his dancing were erratic. The blazing grate and the heated bodies raised the temperature of the Great Room to an uncomfortable degree. The caterwauling of the fiddles and cello pounded in her ears.

It seemed an age before the dancing was over, and the party sat down to a late-night dinner at tables hastily assembled by the servants. Lady Marchbank had gathered her own chums at her table, thus making it impossible for Hartly to join them.

It was while they were eating that Lady Marchbank leaned aside and said to Jonathon, "I see Hartly has skipped out. Now where the deuce could he be? Would you mind taking a scout about to see what he is up to?"

Jonathon excused himself and left at once. Lady Marchbank leaned aside and said to Moira, "Hartly is not among us. Jon has gone to have a look for him."

Moira felt a chill seize her. If worst came to worst and Hartly discovered the smuggling game, she would have to beg him not to report it. If she had any influence with him, she must use it to save the Marchbanks.

Chapter Ten

No one paid much attention to a youngster like Jonathon. He slipped away from the table and upstairs to tap on Hartly's door. When there was no answer, he darted down to the taproom. Seeing no sign of Hartly, he headed for the front door with a wave to Bullion.

"Just going to see if Firefly is bedded down right and tight," he said.

"That's a fine bit o' blood." Bullion grinned. He believed in keeping his smart clients in curl.

Jonathon did go to the stable. He saw that Hartly's curricle and carriage were both in place. The old jade Bullion had hired as a mount stood in her stall, so wherever Hartly was, he must be close by, for he was on foot.

His next destination was the estuary. The weather conspired to lend his search the whiff of danger. A pale sliver of moon shone in a charcoal sky. Ragged clouds hid the glory of the stars. Mist lay low on the ground and over the dark water, which lapped menacingly against the shore. Three fishing smacks were at anchor, but no ships moved through the mist. The moisture-laden air felt soft as a woman's fingers against his skin. Jonathon peered along the shoreline but could see no sign of his quarry. Remembering that a ship had docked behind the inn the night before, he worked his way around to the back. His black slippers moved noiselessly over the soft ground.

The rear of the inn was a jumble of crates and boxes, of dustbins and cast-off lumber. Hartly, or worse—a Gentleman—could be concealed behind any one of them. Jonathon had heard tales of the vicious stunts employed by the Gentlemen in the last century. Stuffed anyone who interfered with them down a rabbit hole headfirst and locked him in with a forked branch between his legs. Even a slit throat was not beyond them. His heart hammered with excitement as he peered around the various mounds of refuse.

He was about to advance when he thought of a better idea. It would be possible to see the rear of the inn from the inside, through the kitchen window. He would go and compliment the foul-tempered Cook, tell her how much he had enjoyed her lobster patties. With this plan to save face, he darted around to the front again.

As he hastened along, he noticed a ladder leaning against the wall. Surely that had not been there when he passed the first time, or he would have noticed it. He glanced up and saw it went to one of the windows. He had caught a thief red-handed! Before he went hollering for help, he stopped a moment to consider which room the ladder was at. It was not his or Moira's, at least.

Theirs were on the other side. This would be either Hartly's, Stanby's, or Ponsonby's. It was the window closest to the rear. Jonathon felt a certain sympathy for anyone preying on Stanby. He would not like to land a poor farmer in jail for lifting that bleater's tiepin.

He crouched behind a thorn bush and watched. E'er long, a smallish pair of legs came out the window, seeking the ladder. The feet were encased in a gentleman's evening slippers. The legs were followed by a body and head that Jonathon soon recognized as Ponsonby's. No one could possibly be afraid of Ponsonby. Jonathon came forth from the bush and said firmly, "Caught you dead to rights, Ponsonby. Hand over whatever you have stolen and I shan't call the constable."

Surprised by the voice, Ponsonby lost his grip and fell the last four feet to the ground. He looked up with a bleary smile.

"Sir David. Good evening to you, sir. Forgot my key on my toilet table when I left my room. Just recovering it. Here we are."

He rose on unsteady legs, dipped into his pocket, and pulled out the key. "Right where I left it. I wonder, now, would you assist me to my room?"

"Disguised, as usual," Jonathon said, shaking his head.

Jonathon assisted him into the inn but let him stagger upstairs by himself. He had more important things to do. He went directly to the kitchen, where a frazzled Maggie was up to her elbows in work.

"I just wanted to compliment you on that excellent dinner," he said, with a winning smile.

Personal thanks from a guest was a new thing

for Maggie Bullion. She had an occasional visit from dissatisfied customers complaining of tough roast beef or sour milk, but never a compliment. After she recovered from her shock, she said, "Why, thankee, sir. That is mighty civil of ye."

He looked around at the loads of dishes piled by the sink. "What a lot of work this is for you, Mrs. Bullion. Just look at those stacks of dishes."

"Aye, and every one of them will be clean before this body hits the tick. Sal, get filling that washbasin."

Wilf came darting in to request a refill of the sweets platter. Jonathon strolled nonchalantly to the tin trays piled with macaroons, tarts, and chantillies to help himself to a macaroon. While the servants worked, he peered out the window into the yard. When his eyes had adjusted to the darkness, he discerned a man moving about, looking into crates and boxes. The man leaned over and lifted up what looked like a large, flat piece of wood roughly three feet square. When the man—it was Hartly—disappeared before his very eyes, Jonathon deduced that the piece of wood was a trapdoor, leading to a storage place for brandy.

He had seen enough. He grabbed up two more macaroons and returned to the Great Hall.

"Hartly is exploring out back," he told Lady Marchbank. "He has found the trapdoor."

Lady Marchbank turned pale. "Pest of a man! It will cost a pretty penny to buy his silence."

She developed a migraine and left very soon after, to report to her husband. "Best give me the sapphires, Moira," she said, before leaving. Moira handed them over.

After seeing Lady Marchbank off, the Trevithicks

remained behind, discussing the matter in low tones.

"There is no doubt in my mind that Hartly is a special agent sent down from London," Jonathon said. "He will have Cousin Vera and Marchbank carried off in chains if we do not stop him."

"He cannot know at this juncture that Marchbank is involved. He will do more spying before he returns to London." And here he let on he was staying only to be with her!

"We must follow him and see what he is up to," Jonathon declared, not without pleasure.

While they were speaking, Hartly came into the room, looking as innocent as a babe. Seeing the empty seat where Lady Marchbank had been sitting, he joined the Trevithicks at the table.

"I just stepped out to blow a cloud," he said. "A lovely evening."

"Yes, I went out for a breath of air myself," Jonathon said. "I was just telling Lady Crieff that I bumped into Ponsonby, drunk as a Dane. He fell off a ladder."

Hartly lifted a satirical eyebrow at Lady Crieff. "I blame it on your giving him that glass of champagne at dinner. I notice you did not offer me one."

"What was he doing on a ladder?" Moira asked, as this was the first she had heard of it.

Jonathon said, "He locked his key in his room. Bullion must have a spare, but he was too disguised to ask for it."

Hartly felt a quiver of interest. Ponsonby had been playing the drunken fool the evening he arrived but had sobered up in the space of a quarter of an hour.

"Which window was he at?" he asked.

"His own, the end one."

"But that is not his room!" Moira exclaimed. "He is across the hall from us. Major Stanby has the end suite."

"By Jove, you are right!" Jonathon said. "But Ponsonby had the key in his pocket. He must have taken Major Stanby's key. I wonder if he was really foxed or only shamming it."

"I shall have a word with him," Hartly said.

"I expect he is in his own room by now," Jonathon said. "P'raps we should remove that ladder from Stanby's window first. It is an invitation to thieves."

"An excellent idea," Hartly agreed.

Moira remained behind while the gentlemen went out, around to the side of the inn. The ladder was gone. "It was there not five minutes ago!" Jonathon declared.

"I believe you, Sir David."

"I daresay Bullion had it moved."

"Very likely."

Jonathon studied Hartly for a moment, then said, "You don't really think so, do you, Mr. Hartly?"

"No, I do not, Sir David. I suspect Mr. Ponsonby moved it himself. He was trying to steal your stepmama's jewelry and got the wrong room."

"Really!"

"I should warn Lady Crieff that Ponsonby is not always as inebriated as he would have us believe."

"You mean he is a common thief? But he is the tip of the ton. He knows all the fine lords and ladies."

"So he says. It is easy to drop famous names when your audience is in no position to challenge you."

"That is true," Jonathon said, chewing back a secret smile. "Why, any of us might not be who we say we are. Even you and I." Jonathon smiled guilelessly, imagining he was being crafty.

Hartly mistrusted that smile. "I?" he asked. "If I were to impersonate someone, it would not be a plain Mr. Hartly. I would make myself a duke."

"I did not mean you were not Mr. Hartly," Jonathon said. "I only meant you might be doing something other than what you say you are doing here."

"Such as?"

Jonathon began to fear he should not have begun this conversation. He shrugged. "How the deuce should I know?"

As there seemed nothing to be gained from this conversation, Hartly said he would go to check up on Ponsonby.

"I shall go with you," Jonathon said at once.

"I would prefer that you deliver my warning to Lady Crieff, Sir David."

They went inside, Jonathon sulking and Hartly in an unsettled mood. What was Ponsonby up to?

Jonathon gave Moira the warning, and also an account of the missing ladder.

"It is odd about the ladder disappearing," Jonathon said. "I shall ask Bullion if he had it removed."

He darted off and had a word with Bullion. When he returned, his eyes were shining with excitement. "Bullion did not move it! Either Hartly moved it himself before he came in, or Ponsonby did it, which means he was not foxed at all."

"It was Hartly, I warrant," Moira said in a hard voice.

She was beginning to see that Hartly cared nothing for her. He was using her relationship with the Marchbanks as an excuse to ferret out information. His insistence that she leave her jewels with them would provide another excuse to visit Cove House. He would offer to accompany her for safety's sake and try to get into the caves while he was there. He already knew of their existence.

She was just discussing her fears with Jonathon when Hartly returned.

"I could get nothing out of Ponsonby," he said. "He was either asleep or doing a good job of shamming it. Perhaps he was foxed, as he was entering the wrong room. Yet it is odd the key he got from Stanby's toilet table fit his own door." He already knew each key was different. He had tried to get into Stanby's room with his own key earlier.

"The key he *said* he got from Stanby's room," Jonathon said, with a knowing look. "He had his own key all the while. He was after something else in Stanby's room."

"It is no secret Stanby is well-to-grass," Hartly said. "I shall warn Bullion that he may possibly be harboring a thief under his roof."

The local guests had left the party. The servants were creating a great ruckus in the clearing of the tables.

"We are in the way here. It is time to retire," Moira said.

Hartly accompanied them abovestairs, urging Moira to take her jewels to her cousin's house for safekeeping.

"I would be happy to accompany you," he said.

Moira and Jonathon exchanged a knowing look. "I was sure you would," Moira said. "So kind of you, but that will not be necessary. If I decide to do as you suggest, I shall ask Cousin John to send his carriage with a couple of armed footmen. It is kind of you to worry about them, but I shan't have them here long in any case."

His dark eyes gleamed with curiosity. "It is not the jewelry that concerns me so much as yourself, Lady Crieff. Er . . . have you decided when you will be leaving, as you mentioned not being here long?" he asked.

Moira tapped his arm with her fan. "Curiosity killed the cat, Mr. Hartly. I did not say I would be leaving. I said my jewelry would not be here. Now there is a puzzle for you to solve."

His curiosity turned to a worried frown. "I trust this puzzle does not involve Major Stanby?"

"I am not likely to take any chances with my jewels," she said vaguely.

"I would not entrust them to—to a stranger," he said. "As David and I were mentioning earlier, a man is not always what he seems."

"How very true," she said, turning to unlock her door, to conceal the involuntary sneer that had seized her lips. Then she turned around, smiling. "Thank you for your escort, Mr. Hartly. Good night."

She opened the door and went in. Jonathon followed her, leaving Hartly alone in the hallway, frowning.

He, like everyone else at the inn, knew her collection was in Bullion's safe. The least he could do was make sure that the safe was a good one and perhaps arrange that someone be on guard in the room at night. He had matters to discuss with Bullion, in any case, and went belowstairs. He discussed the matter of smuggling first. He convinced Bullion to assist him in a certain scheme he was hatching. After he had Bullion's confidence, he mentioned the jewels.

"Did Lady Crieff remember to have her sapphires put away with the rest of her jewels?" he asked. He could not remember whether she had been wearing them when he accompanied her upstairs. He had a vivid memory of her large, silver-gray eyes, which seemed to be laughing at him. He remembered her green gown, and the enticing body in it, but he could not remember seeing the sapphires.

"No, she did not, sir. She'll bring them down tomorrow, I daresay."

"I hope that safe is a good, stout one?"

"That it is, sir."

"May I have a look at it?"

"See for yourself."

He led Hartly into a cubbyhole of an office whose sole furnishings were a large, battered desk and two chairs. "The gentleman you're concerned about would never even find the safe, let alone pry her open."

He pushed the desk aside, lifted the worn carpet, and pointed to a door in the floor, with a sunken handle that allowed the carpet to lie flat. He unlocked the door and lifted it, revealing a box built into the floor. There, along with a tin box containing cash and business papers, sat Lady Crieff's jewelry case. She had not even bothered to lock it when she got out her "sapphires" for the party. These paste stones had been left under her mattress, while she wore her Cousin Vera's genuine stones.

"Would you like to see the jewels?" Bullion asked.

"Indeed I would."

Bullion lifted the lid, revealing a glitter of diamonds, along with colored stones, all arranged in dark blue velvet. At first glance, it looked like a pirate's treasure chest. Bullion took up the green necklace.

"These are the Crieff emeralds," he said in a hushed voice.

Hartly reached out his hand and held them up to the light. He knew at a glance that they were paste. They did not have the glow of genuine stones. The weight and the feel of them were wrong. The setting was well done, but the stones were imperfectly fashioned. An occasional rough edge could be discerned when he ran his fingers around the larger stones. He said nothing to Bullion but laid the emeralds aside and took up a diamond necklace. It, too, was of paste. He looked in vain for the small diamond necklace she had worn the evening she arrived. It was not there.

"Very impressive," he said. "Best put them away."

They were fakes. The entire Crieff collection was made of paste. Was it a clever stunt to fool a potential thief? Were the genuine jewels safely stowed away at Cove House? That was the logical answer. But what if these were the only "jewels" Lady Crieff possessed? Was she unaware they were not genuine? Or did she know it perfectly well and hope to sell them to some uninformed gentleman as the real thing?

His mind was seething with various intrigues. Was it possible that Lady Crieff was nothing but a wicked adventuress? He felt betrayed. After he had left and gone to his room, he discussed the matter with Mott.

"Would it be Stanby she's chosen as her victim?" Mott asked. "It seems they are pretty close."

"She is on dangerous ground if that is her plan. Stanby will not be gulled by a green girl."

"I doubt she is a green girl, Daniel. There would be a sort of poetic justice in it if she conned him, though. I should like to see someone get the better of that bounder."

"You are letting your romantic spirit lead you astray, Rudolph," Hartly said dampingly. "If *she* gets his blunt out of him, where does that leave us?"

"True. We must stop her."

"Our best bet is to rush our own scheme forward. Stanby is interested. I have had a few discussions with him. Bullion is on board as well. I shall arrange a meeting with all the interested parties tomorrow morning in Bullion's office."

"Excellent. Do you know enough about the operation to pull it off?"

"I mean to take another run down to Cove House this evening. You keep an eye on things here. That includes Ponsonby, by the by. He could be trouble. Well, I am off."

Chapter Eleven

"You are right, Jonathon. We must follow Hartly," Moira said, tossing her shawl, evening reticule, and fan onto the bed. "I shall change into my riding habit and meet you in ten minutes. Do not wear your good evening clothes. We cannot afford a rent in them."

"We will be seen leaving the inn," Jonathon pointed out. "It is well enough for me, but for a lady . . ."

"If I had remembered ladies were so restricted in their movements, I would have posed as a young man. Could you bring that ladder around to the window for me?"

"If I can find it. It cannot be far away."

"Best bring the dark lantern from the carriage as well."

They both scrambled out of their good evening clothes and into rougher wear. E'er long, Moira heard a scraping at her window, and after her first leap of fear, she realized it was Jonathon. She opened the window and followed him down the ladder.

"Luckily, the groom was sound asleep. He did not hear me lead Firefly and Gray Lady out."

They mounted and rode out of the inn yard, along the dark highway in pursuit of Mr. Hartly. There was no one on the road at this hour of the night. The nags were good ones, and they urged them on to a gallop as they sped through the night, with the cool breeze fanning their cheeks and the ghostly shadows of trees and bushes menacing them from the encroaching fields. On their other side, the water gleamed darkly. As they approached Cove House, they slowed to a walk to lessen the sound of the horses' hooves. They tethered their mounts in the shadow of a spreading elm outside the gate leading to the house proper. The Gothic spires and finials loomed into the sky. Every pointed window spoke of danger, of ghosts and monsters.

"Let us check out the sea first," Moira whispered. "Cousin John may be landing a load tonight. We must warn him."

They darted toward the shore and peered below. The cove was quiet, the silver water undisturbed by so much as a ripple.

"He brought in a load this afternoon. It seems tonight is safe," Moira said. "Hartly will see nothing, if he is lurking nearby."

They peered all about but could see no sign of him.

Sticking to the shadows, they carefully picked their way back toward the house. "The blue door is on the other side of the house," Jonathon whispered. "I warrant that is where he is."

He led her to the door, which was set on a slant into the wall, just where a flying buttress protruded. Jonathon reached for the door handle.

"Wait!" Moira whispered. "Listen before you go in. Do you have the lantern?" Jonathon held it aloft. "Very likely Cousin John removed the barrels. I told Cousin Vera that Hartly knew of this cave."

When they heard no sound from the cave, Jonathon opened the door, lifted the shutter of the dark lantern, and held it aloft to look into the cavern. A low tunnel, black as pitch, led underground to the caves. The tunnel and caves were above water level, but they were permanently damp.

"This way," Jonathon said, and stepped in.

Moira took one last look about, then lifted her skirt and stepped reluctantly into the gloomy passage.

In the tunnel, Hartly had heard the door opening. The acoustics in the cave magnified sound yet distorted it in some manner that made its source uncertain. He could discern whispers but could not distinguish either the speakers or the direction of the voices. Echoes bounced off walls and ceilings, until he felt it was the cave itself that was whispering to him.

Like everyone else, he had heard rumors of the cutthroat ways of the Gentlemen, when one was foolish enough to interfere with their work. Bullion had assured him the Blaxstead gang was not as vicious as they led folks to believe. He did not fear for his life, but he knew he was in for a thrashing if they caught him.

He looked all about for a hiding place, but the tunnel offered no concealment. It was just a passage hewn out of the rock. His best bet was to remain perfectly still and hope they did not see him. As the cave held no barrels, he assumed the Gentlemen were bringing cargo in. The voices would be coming from the blue door, then, not the caves. He would stay well back from the opening until they left, then leave himself. Soon another fear assailed him. They might lock the door in some manner when there was brandy in the cave. It had been unlocked when he arrived, but it was also empty. If they barred the door behind them, he would have to find an exit by the caves, which would involve swimming.

He stood perfectly still, flat against the wall, with his ears cocked. As the intruders drew closer, he could distinguish that they were coming from the direction of the door. It sounded like only two men approaching. Perhaps he could handle two. He was a fair bruiser. If they had guns, however, a fight might surprise them into shooting. Better to let them pass. If they discovered him, he would just have to do his best. He needed a weapon. He knelt down and felt around the ground for a loose piece of stone or anything he might use. His fingers felt a smooth piece of wood. He picked it up and ran his hands along it to judge its size and strength. It was a sort of rough club, probably used by the Gentlemen and left behind sometime.

He picked it up and curled his fingers around it, ready to strike. As the light of the lantern appeared around the corner, he stared, trying to gauge the strength of his opponents. The first man was as tall as himself. He had to bend over to prevent scraping the ceiling of the cave with his head. His hunched posture concealed his build. The one behind seemed to be shorter.

The lantern cast only a dim light. The man did not move it about to examine the walls as he passed. Hartly let the first man go by. Just as the man passed, he turned his head and looked back at Hartly. He must have seen a shadow, or possibly even have heard a breath. Long experience in Spain told Hartly his best bet was to attack the nearer man first. He lifted his club and landed the second fellow a sharp blow on the side of the head. The fellow gave one groan and toppled over. The man who had already passed ran to help his comrade. Hartly took advantage of his brief reprieve to flee the cave.

Once he had gained the safety of the outdoors, he did not waste a moment. He ran toward the park, hopped onto his waiting jade, and disappeared into the shadows of the night. He would hasten to check out the barn before the men in the cave had time to warn the others.

In the cave, Jonathon looked at the fleeing form, uncertain whether to give chase or tend to Moira, who was moaning at his feet. His imagination preferred the heroic role of giving chase, but reality was less frightening—and besides, Moira might be hurt badly.

"Are you all right?" he asked, leaning over and holding up the lantern to examine her.

A trickle of what looked like molasses, but was of course blood, oozed slowly down the side of her temple.

"Was it him? Was it Hartly?" she asked.

"I did not get much of a look at him, but it could have been."

"It must have been," she said, struggling to her feet.

Jonathon assisted her. "I shall take you to Cousin Vera. P'raps you ought to let a sawbones take a look at your head."

"No, we do not want to bother her at this hour of the night. Lend me your handkerchief, Jonathon."

She took it and dabbed at her wound. It hurt, but it was by no means serious enough to require a doctor.

When Jonathon was sure she was not dying, he said, "I have just thought of something else. If Hartly returns directly to the inn, he will see our mounts are gone."

"I doubt he will return at once. He is out scouting for evidence. He will examine the stables and ditches and haystacks while he is here. If we hurry, we might beat him back."

They left the tunnel and hastened back to their mounts. Moira half expected that Hartly would have stolen them, but they were quietly champing the grass under the elm tree. They rode back to Blaxstead. Jonathon put up the ladder, and Moira ascended to her room. When she was safely in, Jonathon took the mounts to the stable. He returned the ladder to the back of the house where he had found it and went into the inn by the front door, which was, fortunately, on the latch. He scampered quickly upstairs and went to Moira's room.

He found his sister at the dim mirror, washing the blood from her head.

"Look at me!" she exclaimed in chagrin. "How am I to explain this bruise tomorrow?"

"Say you bumped into a door," Jonathon replied, going to take a closer peek at it. "Does it hurt much?"

"It is tender," she said. "But I do not mind that. Of more importance, we must get word to Cousin John at once that Hartly is investigating him."

"You mean tonight?"

"No, first thing in the morning. You must be up at first light and ride to Cove House. Tell Cousin John what happened in the tunnel. He will know what to do. I daresay it will amount to no more than discontinuing his operations until Hartly has left."

This was a task much to Jonathon's liking. It had the desired air of intrigue without the actual danger of being shot or beaten up.

"I'll do it. And I shall keep an eye to the keyhole tonight to see when Hartly returns as well. I should not be surprised if he stops off for a word with Ponsonby. I doubt that an inspector would be sent down without a few helpers. Mott is likely another of them. He acts pretty havey-cavey for a valet. I have seen him poking about hayricks and ditches, looking for brandy. Hartly has Ponsonby posing as a drunkard and Mott as a fool to give them a harmless air."

"You could be right. But then that leaves us with another question. What was Ponsonby doing in Stanby's room? Is it possible they are all working together?"

"Stanby working on the side of the law?" Jonathon scoffed. "Not likely. We have no notion what is going on, Moira. We have got to find out, for Cousin John's sake. I believe I shall get out the ladder again and have a go at Hartly's room while he is out."

"Oh, no, Jon. You are forgetting his valet. Mott will not retire until his master returns. He will be in the next room."

"So he will. I quite forgot."

Moira liked the idea of spying on Hartly and was loath to give it up. "But we might do it tomorrow, when they are both out," she said. "Mott does not spend his entire day in his room. We shall stick close to the inn. My wound will provide a good excuse. When they are both out, we shall figure out a way to get into Hartly's room."

This plan pleased Jonathon. He went off to bed, mentally figuring out means of access to a locked room, for of course he could not use the ladder in broad daylight. He knew the female servants. Sally and Sukey carried the keys when they were making up the guests' rooms. Sally was a friendly sort of chit. He might con her into lending him her keys.

Jonathon and Moira were both sound asleep at three o'clock when Hartly returned to his room. His "valet" was by no means so conscientious as he led folks to believe. He, too, was sawing logs. Hartly could discuss his doings only silently with himself.

He poured a glass of claret and proceeded to do this. It would be impossible to give Stanby a tour of the tunnel and caves if there were Gentlemen about. He had to find some way of bringing the smuggling operations to a temporary halt. Bullion might be useful there. A hint that there was a senior Revenue officer down from London looking into the lack of arrests at Blaxstead might work. He counted on Stanby's greed to do the rest. Lady

Crieff might be troublesome there. Hartly was quite sure she had fingered Stanby as her victim, and there was no saying his pockets were deep enough to be fleeced by them both.

A soft smile lifted his lips. He was not overly concerned about Lady Crieff now that he knew her "jewels" were composed of paste. He had only to drop a hint, and the hoyden would no doubt take her collection to some other out-of-the-way spot and start over again. His smile dwindled to a frown as he considered her connection to the Marchbanks. They could not know what the hussy was up to. They seemed to have a genuine fondness for the chit. As a last resort, her attempted fraud might be used to keep Marchbank in line, if he proved troublesome.

But still his frown remained, growing deeper as other thoughts slipped from his mind and the image of Lady Crieff took hold. She was so young to be headed down the road to ruin. Even without a dowry, she might make a good match. A lady's face had proved an effectual fortune before now. With the Marchbanks to lend her countenance, there was no reason she could not marry respectably. It would be a kindness to hint her in that direction. Yet the notion of that enchanting creature shackled to some country squire did not entirely please him either.

He finished his wine and went to bed.

Chapter Twelve

The small plaster over Lady Crieff's left eye was not disfiguring, but it was noticeable enough to cause talk when she appeared in the Great Room the next morning. Mr. Hartly, in particular, stared at it in alarm. It couldn't be! Lady Crieff had no reason to be in the tunnel last night. It could only be a coincidence. Yet one of the men had been noticeably small, the other tall, like David. Good lord, had he inadvertently beaten a lady?

Major Stanby was the first to offer his sympathy. He had come down to breakfast early and was leaving the room as Lady Crieff and Sir David entered.

"My dear Lady Crieff! What happened? I trust you were not seriously hurt!"

"A mere bump, Major. I left the door of my clothespress ajar and walked into it last night. One is not accustomed to such cubbyholes of rooms."

"I hope you called in a doctor. A bump on the head can be serious," he said, all concern.

"I would not let a country sawbones near me,"

she said scornfully. "I patched myself up, with David's help."

"I am happy to hear it is not serious. Still, it is a shame to have even a millimeter of that exquisite face covered," he said, gazing at her with his gooseberry eyes until she wanted to scream.

She simpered. "Too kind."

"You must take it easy today. A quiet read by the grate. I shall be happy to bear you company this afternoon. I shall dart out this moment and see what magazines are available in the shops to amuse you."

She thanked him and continued toward her table. Ponsonby was the next one to offer sympathy.

"Milady! What ill has befallen you? I tremble at the sight of that plaster—and on your face, too. Why could you not have bumped your elbow? A bruise there could easily be hidden by a judicious arrangement of the shawl."

"Why, Mr. Ponsonby, you give me the idea you are interested only in a lady's appearance," she said coolly.

"Until I have had the pleasure of plumbing your soul, madam, I can take my pleasure only in admiring your exquisite beauty."

"Even for looking it is always preferable to be sober, is it not?" she said, shaking an admonitory finger. "I am very angry with you, sir."

He scowled at Jonathon. "You told her!" Then he turned back to Moira. "It is true I was bottle-bitten last night, but I place the blame in your dish, madam. The pain of seeing you dancing with other gentlemen . . ."

"Strange it should lead you to go climbing ladders."

"No, no, it led me straight to the bottle, to drown my woes."

"You are easily led astray," she said, and brushed past him to take her seat at the table.

Ponsonby just smiled and went tailing off after Stanby.

Hartly sat on alone, brooding over his coffee. Was it Lady Crieff he had assaulted last night in the tunnel? Of equal importance, had she recognized him? It had been extremely dark. He had not recognized her, so it was not likely she had recognized him. To ignore her plaster when the others were making such a fuss over it would appear odd, yet the hypocrisy of lamenting his own ill deed left a bad taste in his mouth.

After she had been seated, he rose and went to her table.

"Lady Crieff, David," he said with a bow. "I am sorry to see you have injured yourself, milady. I hope it is not serious?"

"A mere scratch," she replied, then added, "but it is very painful," for she wanted him to know he had hurt her. "Won't you join us, Mr. Hartly? I see you are finished breakfast, but you can take your coffee with us."

"Are you well enough to go for a drive?" he asked, sitting down, but not bothering to bring his cup.

"The major suggests I take it easy today, and I feel he is right, for my head does ache dreadfully. He has offered to keep me company by the grate."

Hartly disliked that mention of Stanby, but he was more worried to hear she was still suffering from her blow. "Perhaps you ought to call in a doctor."

"If it persists, I shall. Meanwhile I have taken a

headache powder and shall just stick about the inn."

"Then I shall know where to find you when I have finished my correspondence. I have a few letters to write home regarding my estate."

"You are staying in this morning, then?" Jonathon asked.

Hartly noticed the quick look the pair exchanged, and he wondered at it. He soon deduced that David was hinting for a ride in his curricle. He decided to oblige him, to atone for last night.

"My letter writing will not take long. Would you like to have a spin in my curricle later, around eleven?"

"I cannot leave Lady Crieff alone," he said, with the utmost reluctance, "but I should love to do it another time."

"Tomorrow, then."

Hartly took his leave and went abovestairs. His main concern was that he was the cause of Lady Crieff's headache. It was not until he was at his desk that he began wondering why Sir David had refused the ride when it was plain as a pikestaff that he wanted to go. The major had offered to accompany Lady Crieff on the settee in front of the grate. There would be servants and the Bullions about. Surely she did not require young David to dance attendance all day.

"You are staying in this morning, then?" David had asked, with a sharp look about him. It almost suggested they wanted him out of his room. They would know that Mott always took a morning constitutional. Did they plan to sneak into his room? Was that it? What did they hope to find? He had brought nothing incriminating with him, but it soon occurred to him that this was an excellent way to make Marchbank think he was a special Revenue agent from London. He would already suspect it if the Crieffs reported his visit to the cave.

He scribbled off a note to an imaginary Mr. Giles of the Revenue and Customs Department, crossed half of it out, squeezed it into a ball, and tossed it in the dustbin. Then he did his real correspondence and took his letters belowstairs.

Lady Crieff and Sir David had removed to the settee, where they sat with their heads together, talking in a low, confidential manner. When David spotted him, he said something to his stepmama, and they both stopped talking.

Hartly made a detour to the settee before leaving. "I am just stepping out to post these letters, while I have my walk," he said. "Can I do anything for you while I am out, Lady Crieff? More headache powders?"

"I am well supplied, thank you. I hope you enjoy your walk."

"I plan to stroll eastward. Mott was going to walk to Cove House today. He is interested in Gothic architecture. I shall meet him on his way back."

"He must have left early," Moira said.

"Yes, as soon as he had shaved me. I was up early today, to look over my dairy accounts before breakfast. Well, I am off."

"Enjoy your walk," Lady Crieff said.

As soon as he was out of the inn, Moira said, "This is our chance, Jonathon. He will be gone an hour at least. Cove House is over five miles away. Let us go upstairs at once."

She leaned on Jonathon's arm, to lend credibility

to her headache. Bullion was all solicitude and apologized for his clothespress door.

"It is my own fault. I was careless," Moira said.

The girls were making up the beds when they went abovestairs. Sally was just coming out of Hartly's room. Before she locked the door, Jonathon called to her and she came to him.

"Lady Crieff is going to have a lie-down," he said.

Sally curtsied. "Yes, sir. Her room is all made up. I shan't disturb her."

"Good lass. And would you mind trotting downstairs and getting a posset for her? She could not eat a bite of breakfast."

"Yes, sir, right away, sir." She curtsied again and darted down the back staircase.

Jonathon gave a cagey grin. "She forgot to lock Hartly's door. Excellent. I shall just wait about to make sure she don't lock it when she brings the posset. There is no need for you to look out for Hartly. He will be gone an hour at least. There is no sign of rain to send him running back for cover."

"I shall go to his room with you. Two sets of eyes are better than one."

Jonathon did as he had said. When Sally returned with the posset, he went to the top of the stairs to meet her and chatted in a friendly way to keep her mind off Hartly's door.

"Are you from this neighborhood?" he asked.

"Born and bred right here in Blaxstead. My da runs the cobbler's shop. You might have seen it on the high street."

"No, but, by Jove, I shall stop in and have him hammer down this nail that has come up through my boot. It is digging into my heel."

"Tell him I sent you and he'll do it for free." She smiled.

"I shall do that. Well, I must not keep you from your work." He handed her a small coin.

Even as they spoke, Maggie's voice came traveling up the backstairs, hollering for Sally. Sally gave a bold smile and trotted off. Jonathon rushed the posset along to Moira, who set it on the table. They opened the door, peered out to check that the hall was empty, then went along to Hartly's room.

It was clear at a glance that Mott was an excellent valet. There was not so much as a soiled cravat or handkerchief to mar the tidiness of the chamber.

"You check the clothespress. I shall look in the desk," Moira said.

Jonathon went to the clothespress and began looking through pockets. They were empty; not so much as a comb or a stray penny had been left behind. There was not even any lint. All he learned was that the clothing was nearly new and of an enviable quality. A set of silver brushes sat on the toilet table, along with shaving equipment and a jewelry box holding a small diamond cravat pin, the one Hartly had worn the night before. The drawers of the dresser held clean linen and socks.

Moira fared no better. The desk held a few recent journals, but no significant articles were circled to give her a clue what he had been reading. If Hartly had brought an address book, he had not left it here. The blotting pad had not been changed for months. Remnants of blotted words ran higgledy-piggledy into each other, completely illegible.

"You would hardly think anyone had been living in this room at all," Moira said in disgust when they compared notes. "There is not a single personal item to give us a clue. Such care in covering his tracks seems highly suspicious. Take a quick peek in Mott's room, Jon. I shall search under the mattress and pillow. People often hide things there."

Jonathon went to Mott's room, which was in a state similar to Hartly's. It held nothing of interest. When he returned, Moira was just poking into the dustbin.

"Here is something!" she exclaimed, pulling out a piece of crumpled paper.

She straightened it out and read what had been written. "It is true!" she gasped. "He is a spy for Revenue and Customs! Listen to this, Jon. 'I wish to report that I have been executing my orders and have some small success to report. I believe a Lord Marchbank, of Cove House, is responsible for the large quantity of brandy that is entering England illegally at Blaxstead. He is also the local magistrate. No smugglers have been convicted here for a decade. I shall continue surveillance to discover the entire operation, and keep in touch.' He has crossed out the next bit. It is difficult to read—something about sending more men down."

Jonathon dashed to read this startling news for himself. "We must warn Cousin John!" he exclaimed.

"Yes, certainly. And it was Hartly who hit me last night. I knew it was him."

"Let us go," he said. "Take the letter to show Marchbank."

Moira looked at it doubtfully. "He might notice it is gone."

"Sally has done the room. He will think she emptied the basket."

Moira stood, undecided. It might be a trap. Hartly was so devious, she could hardly believe he had left this incriminating piece of evidence behind by accident.

"We can tell Cousin John what it says. I shall leave it here."

"What a good idea," Mr. Hartly said, in a voice of quiet menace.

She turned at the sound of his voice. He had entered by Mott's room and stood in the doorway, staring at her with a smile that was more deadly than a charged pistol.

"Mr. Hartly!" she gasped. Her blood turned to ice water, chilling her to the core. She felt frozen to the spot, unable to move. "What are you doing here?"

He advanced slowly, with measured strides. "I live here, for the time being. More to the point, what are you and Sir David doing here, Lady Crieff?" he asked, studying her with a fixed stare. "I believe you have some explaining to do."

Chapter Thirteen

Hartly had seen that dumb, animal response to danger in Spain. The frozen faces of the enemy at bay still haunted his dreams. That was Lady Crieff's reaction when he caught her in his room. But it was the look in her eyes that bothered him more. It was the same fear and loathing he had seen when she looked at Stanby. He felt like a murderer.

"Well?" he said gruffly. "Nothing to say, madam? You mistook my room for yours, perhaps? You were passing and heard a noise? Fearing a robber, you came to investigate. Come now, use that vivid imagination."

She swallowed; her tongue flicked out and touched her dry lips. "It was the door—it was open," she said. She still held the note in her fingers, hidden behind her back. She wanted to position herself over the dustbin and drop it in.

"Ah, you have elected for excuse number two."

Jonathon came to her defense. "The door was

open!" he said angrily. "We knew you were out walking and feared someone might steal your—your diamond tiepin."

"And did someone?" he asked.

"No! You can look for yourself. It is still on your dresser."

Hartly's eyes flickered to the dresser, where his diamond cravat pin twinkled in the sunlight. Well, at least they had not robbed him. Lady Crieff's position at the desk told him what they had been looking for. So they had read the note he left for them. Excellent! Success mellowed his mood. He would let them off lightly, but not too lightly, or they would suspect his motives.

Jonathon's spunky behavior gave Moira courage. She shifted position and dropped the note into the dustbin. Once free of the incriminating evidence, she lifted her head high and said haughtily, "I hope you are not accusing us of trying to rob you, Mr. Hartly, when we were only being neighborly. The door was open, I assure you. Anyone might have come in. You can ask Sally."

"You must forgive me," he said, in a more civil tone. "I was surprised when I returned and heard voices in my room, especially after Ponsonby's questionable behavior last night. I decided to enter via Mott's room to catch the intruder. It was careless of Sally to leave the door open. I shall speak to her."

"I wish you will be easy with her," Jonathon said. "It was my fault in a way. I asked her for a posset for Lady Crieff just as she was coming out of your room. I daresay that was what made her forget."

"No harm done."

"We thought you were going for a long walk, you see," Jonathon mentioned.

"So I was, but I remembered I had accepted an invitation to dinner in London on the weekend, and returned to write my apologies to the hostess."

"We shall let you get on with it," Moira said, for she was eager to escape. "I am sorry if we startled you."

"Please do not apologize. I ought to thank you for looking out for my welfare."

He accompanied them to the door and watched as they scuttled off to their rooms as if the hounds of hell were after them. As soon as they disappeared, he went to his dustbin and glanced down at the note. It had been opened and obviously read. He strolled to the window and waited to see which of them darted the note's contents off to Marchbank. Within two minutes David ran to the stable and came out, leading Firefly. His simple plan had succeeded. Marchbank would believe his men were being watched and would desist operations for a few nights.

In her room, Moira was trembling from the aftermath of her ordeal. She saw that future relations with Mr. Hartly would be strained and unpleasant, which was a great pity, because in the worst case, she had thought she could apply to him for leniency on Cousin John's behalf. Quite apart from that, she did care for his good opinion. What must he think of her?

She was so upset that she remained in her room the rest of the morning. Jonathon was soon back from Cove House.

"I gave Cousin Vera the message. Marchbank was out on business, but she will tell him. She says he can divert any incoming cargo to Cousin Peter's men at Romney. They have a system of warning lights flashed from shore to the approaching ships. I am to keep watch on Hartly," he said, his chest swelling at such an important duty.

"You did well, Jon. Do you think Hartly believed us?"

"No, he thinks we are common thieves. You could see it in his eyes, but as his precious diamond pin was still there, he could not say much. I doubt he will offer me a ride in his curricle again," he added disconsolately.

"Never mind, you can set up your own curricle when we recover our money. That is the main thing. We must not lose track of that with Cousin John's problem."

"Can I really? With a pair of matched grays like Hartly's? And a yellow rig with silver appointments?"

"Why not? You have earned it."

Moira found her own good advice hard to take. It was difficult to concentrate on Lionel March. She kept remembering the cold way Mr. Hartly had looked at her. She could not face the Great Room for lunch. She kept brooding over Mr. Hartly. She had a cold collation brought to the sitting room, where she and Jonathon shared a quiet luncheon. After lunch, Jonathon planned to watch Hartly and follow him at a discreet distance if he left the inn. He also spoke of taking another run down to Cove House, to see if he could be of any help to Cousin John.

Moira had to take herself by the scruff of the neck and force herself to go belowstairs, where she knew Major Stanby would look for her. She felt the time was ripe to try to sell him the jewels. The settee was empty when she entered the Great Room. The servants had cleared away the traces of lunch. The only person in the room was an elderly gentleman, a traveler, reading a magazine at one of the tables while he sipped coffee.

Moira picked up a journal and sat staring at it with unseeing eyes. Within a quarter of an hour, she heard the firm tread of Lionel March, and her spine stiffened. She forced a smile of welcome when he came bowing and scraping forward.

"I was concerned when you did not come down for luncheon, Lady Crieff," he said, lifting his coat-tails and sitting closer to her than she liked. "I hope the headache is not worse?"

The major had made a dashing run to Dover, where he had spent an hour at the newspaper office, looking into the history of Lady Crieff. He was now in full possession of all the details, including the value of the Crieff collection.

"Truth to tell, Major, it was something else that was bothering me. The jeweler from London should be here by now. I begin to wonder if he has changed his mind, after having me come all this way to meet him. I don't know what I shall do if he does not come."

"Have you thought over my offer?"

She gave a small, trusting smile. "You are so kind, but truly I could not let the jewels out of my possession for only five thousand pounds. They are worth twenty times that. Who is to say you would not be robbed on your way to Paris? I shall just take them to London and try my luck there."

"If you mistrust me—and you are quite right to

mistrust a stranger's ingenuity, if not his honesty—you could come to France with me," he said.

She gave a gasp of alarm. "Major Stanby! I could not travel about with a gentleman! What would people think?"

"You misunderstand me, my dear. I meant you could hire a chaperon and accompany me. In that manner, you would see I do not plan to run off with your fortune." He gave a disparaging laugh at such an idea. "Have you ever been to Paris?"

"No, I have never even been to London."

"You were made for Paris, and Paris for you. It is delightful."

She had to talk this idea away and said, "I do not speak French. I would not be comfortable there. I would prefer to deal with an honest Englishman."

Stanby shook his head doubtfully. "I do not wish to add to your troubles, my dear, but if the jeweler has not come, there must be a reason for it. It is very difficult to sell jewels of—how shall I put it—doubtful origin. Jewels that the law might say are stolen, even though they are yours by rights."

"But that is why I was willing to sell them for half their value. I am aware that they would be difficult to sell in the short term. Eventually the talk will die down. I shall write to Mr. Everett, the jeweler. Do you think I ought to lower my price?" she asked uncertainly. "He might come for forty thousand."

"You would be fortunate to get ten for them, milady."

"Ten thousand! But that is ludicrous. Aubrey's lawyers would settle for more than that, to avoid going to court. They spoke of giving me a fifth of the value, twenty thousand pounds. If I cannot do better than that, I shall take them back to Penworth."

Stanby was happy with the figure. He patted her hand gently. "I see you are shrewd as well as pretty. I have a broad circle of acquaintances from my business dealings in London. I might know a collector who would give you a little more than twenty. Just between ourselves, what would you take?"

"Thirty," she said, knowing there must be some haggling but determined not to take less than the twenty-five March had stolen from her and Jonathon.

He frowned. "I doubt Lord—my friend would go that high. Let me offer him the collection for twenty-five and see what he says."

"Only a quarter of their worth? I had hoped to get more. Oh, very well. I suppose I must, as I am at my wit's end."

"Of course, I would have to see the jewels. I daresay my friend would trust me to act as his agent in the matter. We are old and true friends."

Moira felt a suffocating excitement invade her. She could hardly speak for the blood pounding in her ears. She was on the verge of success, and she must deal most cautiously or all her work was in vain. March knew her face now; there would be no second chance. The first item was to show the jewels in a poor light. In daylight, he would see they were fakes.

"You have seen one set of diamonds, and the sapphires," she reminded him.

"It is the emeralds, however, that are most valuable, I believe. I wonder you did not wear them with that enchanting green gown last night."

"They are much too valuable to be flaunting at a

public inn. But I shall wear them this evening so that you may judge them," she said.

"Excellent. You shall dine with me, Lady Crieff, to allow me to study them a little."

She gave an insouciant smile. "Good gracious, Major, do you not trust me?" she asked. "I have admitted I do not have full legal entitlement to the collection, but I assure you the jewels are genuine. I can show you articles from the journals, if you do not believe me. They were quite horrid about it, but even the most scurrilous hack did not suggest the jewels were fakes. Why would the lawyers make such a fuss over paste jewels?"

Her naive arguments convinced Stanby that she had the goods right enough. His next ploy was to firm up a future alliance with her.

"We must keep in touch when you go to London, my dear. A lady possessing twenty-five thousand pounds will attract every gazetted fortune hunter in town. You will require a protector. I have a broad circle of acquaintances. I would be delighted to sponsor you into society."

She smiled fatuously. "Would you really, Major? I was a trifle concerned about how I should meet the right sort of people."

"I would be honored, my dear." He took her fingers and squeezed them warmly. "You and I shall deal very well together."

"What part of town should I live in?" she asked, quelling the urge to withdraw her fingers.

For half an hour they discussed such things as living arrangements and Lady Crieff's debut into society. The major recommended a house close to his own, allegedly on Grosvenor Square. It was not of a presentation at St. James's Court or society balls that he spoke but of such low amusements as the Pantheon masquerades and Vauxhall. Moira expressed a suitable enthusiasm for them all.

"How soon do you think you can be in touch with your friend about selling the jewels?" she asked.

"I shall dash him off a note this very minute. Send it by special messenger. And you will remember you are dining with me this evening, Lady Crieff."

"I look forward to it, Major."

Moira drew a deep breath of relief as she watched him go. The tension eased out of her shoulders, leaving her limp. She felt soiled from such prolonged contact with Lionel March. And she still had to face dinner with him, knowing he was assessing a set of paste emeralds. She must distract him as much as possible. Flirtation seemed the likeliest way to do it—that, and a very low-cut gown. Worst of all, she had to carry out this disgusting charade under the eyes of Mr. Hartly. Her twenty-five thousand pounds were being hard-earned.

Chapter Fourteen

"What did Hartly do this afternoon?" Moira asked Jonathon when he returned to change for dinner.

"He was riding about the countryside, poking into ditches and haystacks and barns looking for brandy. Then he sat on the cliff with a spyglass, watching the smuggling ships for a bit. When he returned to the inn and went into the taproom, I took a run down to Cove House. Cousin John tells me he has brandy hidden all over the countryside. If Hartly moves tonight, he will recover some of the cargo, but he will not be able to tie Marchbank to it. Cousin John means to lie low."

"That is the main thing, that Marchbank not be arrested. He will have to suffer the loss in silence."

"That is what Marchbank said. I am to continue watching Hartly." He looked at his sister and said, "I say, Moira, why are you wearing the emeralds?"

"Major Stanby wants to see them. He has taken

the bait, Jon," she said, and laughed a nervous laugh.

"By the living jingo! Tell me all about it."

She outlined her afternoon's work. "We are to dine at his table this evening," she said in finishing her tale.

"Well done! I wonder you could bear to let the old goat touch you. I should rinse myself off with bleach if I was you. Do you think he will know the stones are paste?"

"God only knows. If he asks me to take them off and looks at them under a loupe, we are lost. I shall just have to claim Sir Aubrey left me a box of strass glass and depart with my tail between my legs. Run along and change. It is nearly time for dinner."

The major wore the smile of a suitor when he met Moira and Jonathon at the door of the Great Room. His eyes went straight to the necklace even before he looked at her face. Expecting to see a fabulous emerald necklace, he found no fault with the stones.

Moira put her hand on his arm and began speaking at once, to distract him. She said in a low voice, "Say nothing in front of David. He does not know of my plan. Did you write that letter to your friend?" she asked.

"Indeed I did. It is on its way to London. We will have an answer by morning."

She spoke more loudly then, including Jonathon in the conversation. "Shall we take our seats?"

The major led her proudly to his table, holding to her arm as if she were a prisoner, which was exactly how she felt.

"I shall sit next to you, Major," she said with a bright smile. He would not have such a good view of the necklace from her side as he would if she sat across from him.

Stanby drew her chair and they all sat down.

Stanby said, "I have ordered champagne, knowing it is a treat for you youngsters."

"David may have only one glass. That will leave the rest for us, Major," she added, smiling flirtatiously.

The champagne was brought and poured.

The sight that greeted Hartly's eyes when he arrived was Lady Crieff and the major, sitting side by side, laughing and sipping champagne, while David was completely ignored. Hartly could not make heads or tails of it. Lady Crieff spoke of mistrusting Stanby. Why had she elected to make a special friend of him? He bowed stiffly, then took up his own seat.

He already knew Lady Crieff's jewels were paste. If she knew it, too, then she might be making a play for a wealthy bachelor. She could hardly have chosen worse than Stanby. It was only her fortune he was after. Yet she was in no real danger; the worst Stanby could do was relieve her of her paste jewels. It might prove a salutary lesson for her. Having settled this, he hoped to forget the matter.

But his mind would not leave him alone. It was aggravating to see her flirting her head off with that old goat of a Stanby. Good God, had she no taste, no scruples at all? Having sold herself to one old man, was she about to repeat her folly?

By dint of outrageous flirtation, Moira managed to keep Stanby from making too close an examination of the "emeralds." Every time his hateful gooseberry eyes turned to look at them, she set up a new round of flirtation. She touched his hand, she smiled and chattered and teased, she leaned forward to let her gown reveal a little more of her bosoms, and generally behaved like a hoyden. All this kept the major in spirits but so annoyed Hartly that he left halfway through his dinner.

Jonathon gobbled down his mutton and said, "May I be excused, Lady Crieff? I have had enough dinner. I would like to go for a ride before it comes on dark."

"Very well, David, but be back before dark."

Stanby turned and seized her fingers. "Alone, at last," he said in dulcet tones.

Moira's heart rose to her throat. What would come next? She never thought she would be happy to see Mr. Ponsonby, but when he stopped at their table, she was so relieved, she greeted him like a lost-lost friend. She teased him about how much he had drunk and asked if Bow Street had discovered him yet.

"Did you know Mr. Ponsonby is a murderer, Major Stanby?" she asked.

"I have heard the tale of Noddy." Stanby smiled.

"Are you on for a friendly game this evening, Major?" Ponsonby inquired. "We missed our game last night because of the assembly."

"Later, Ponsonby. Lady Crieff and I plan a tête-à-tête by the fireside first."

Stanby was smiling at Lady Crieff and missed the brief flash of intelligent interest that shone in Ponsonby's eyes. Moira caught it and wondered if Ponsonby was as foolish as he let on. His loose smile hardened to cynicism. Then, so quickly that she was not sure she had not imagined it, his stupid expression was back in place.

"Do I smell April and May?" he asked coyly.

"You are too foolish," Moira scoffed.

"Business, Ponsonby. Purely business," the major said. "We shall meet around, say, nine? I look forward to it. See if you can round up Hartly as well. I am feeling lucky tonight." He directed a telling look at Moira on the last sentence.

Ponsonby wandered out the door and on outside for a stroll. He spotted Hartly standing alone, gazing balefully at the water, and joined him. "I have just had a word with Stanby," he said. "He is keen for a game later. Are you on?"

"Yes, why not?"

"You noticed who Lady Crieff was dining with? Something brewing there, eh? Romance, do you think, or business?"

"I doubt there is much distinction in their minds."

"I teased them a little. He claimed it was just business."

"If the lady plans to sell him her paste gems, someone ought to warn the bleater." His concern had nothing to do with Stanby's welfare. He was afraid there was not enough money for him to be conned twice.

"You think the collection is not genuine?" Ponsonby asked.

"I know it."

"I did wonder how she got hold of it."

"Getting hold of it was no problem. Sir Aubrey left it to her in his will."

"Oh, no," Ponsonby said, smiling from ear to ear. "He left it to Lady Crieff. The raven-haired beauty is not Lady Crieff. I visited my aunt at Rye this afternoon. She has a sister in Scotland. She tells me Lady Crieff is a bran-faced, red-haired gel, dirt common. Strangely, the real Lady Crieff did take the collection and make a bolt for it. She was caught at the border and hauled back. The story was hushed up for the sake of the family. Auntie heard Lady Crieff settled for ten thousand and has taken up with the head groom. Interesting, eh?"

Hartly stood like a statue, staring in disbelief while a dozen questions buzzed through his head. He gave tongue to the most pressing of them. "But if she is not Lady Crieff, who the devil is she?"

"A dashed pretty adventuress."

"Lady Marchbank acknowledges her."

"That is another odd thing. My aunt has never heard of any connection between the Marchbanks and the Crieffs, and she has known the Marchbanks from the egg. No, Hartly, the hussy read the story somewhere and decided to make gain of it. What I have been puzzling over is the Marchbank connection. How did she bribe or con the Marchbanks into lending her countenance?"

"I have no idea," Hartly replied in a stunned voice.

"And why did she choose Stanby and no one else as her victim? I mean to say, I have been acting the rich fool, throwing myself at her head, and she did not try to sell me her collection of paste. Or you, come to that. You are not entirely indifferent, I think. Why him?"

A slow smile moved across Hartly's lips. "I don't know, but I shall ask her."

Ponsonby frowned. "What, just come right out and ask her? She will lie her head off."

"She hasn't much choice but to give an explanation. I shall insist on it."

"I shouldn't like to do that. I mean to say, she may not be Lady Crieff, but she is a lady, don't you think?"

"Either a provincial lady or a damned fine actress. While we are speaking of explanations, Ponsonby, just what the devil are you really doing here? A man don't hide in Blaxstead when he has killed his man. He rusticates at his estate. There has been no mention of that duel in the journals."

"I daresay Noddy recovered. He was not a bad fellow. I am happy for it, to tell the truth."

"The truth? We have not heard much of that. Come now, I know you were in Stanby's room last night."

"I was bosky."

"No, my friend, you were as sober as you were the night you arrived. I do not think you and I are at odds. I suspect we have something in common, and I could use a colleague."

Ponsonby thought a moment, then said, "Say you are right, just for the sake of argument—what did you have in mind?"

Hartly looked around to see they were not overheard. "There are too many ears here to suit me. Let us walk along a little. I have a story—and a proposition—that might amuse you, Mr. Ponsonby. Or should I say Lord Everly?"

"How the devil did you know that?"

"I did not know it. It was my man, Mott, who recognized you. You were at Harrow with Mott some years ago. You might remember him better by the name Lord Rudolph Sinclair."

"So it *is* Rudy! I thought he looked very like, but it was so many years ago. What the deuce is going on, Hartly?"

"That is what I am about to tell you."

They turned and walked off, away from the small throng around the estuary.

Chapter Fifteen

Jonathon found scant entertainment in following Mr. Hartly from the dining room to the estuary, but that was the extent of the gentleman's travel. Soon Ponsonby had joined up with Hartly, and the two began a dull promenade back and forth along the banks of the water. It was difficult to follow them at a distance that made eavesdropping possible. Ponsonby had given him a couple of decidedly odd looks when he tried it. In the end, Jon was forced to give up. He decided to take Firefly for a ride. When he returned half an hour later, he knew he had not missed a thing, for Ponsonby and Hartly were still at it, talking six to the dozen. Jon stabled his mount and returned to the front door just as they were entering the inn.

"We shall get hold of Stanby and see if he is ready for that game," Ponsonby said.

"You go ahead and get things ready," Hartly replied. "I must have a word with Mott. Tell Bullion it will be just the three of us for cards this evening.

The locals only play for chicken stakes. Perhaps he has a small room he might let us use, somewhere we can play without being disturbed."

When they entered the inn, Hartly cast one long, dark look at the couple by the grate before going abovestairs. Jonathon did likewise. He felt a pang to see Moira still sitting with March. Jon, who knew her so well, could see her nerves were stretched to nearly the breaking point. She looked vastly relieved when Ponsonby called March away for the game, and Jon took his place on the settee.

"You look as if you had been gnawed by rats, Lady Crieff," he said ruefully. "Have you had a wretched time of it?"

"Unspeakably vile. He kept touching me," she said, with a shiver of revulsion. "But it was worth it. I must go to my room to recuperate. A whole box of headache powders could not ease my migraine. You have Bullion put my emeralds in the safe, Jonathon." She removed the necklace and ear pendants and handed them to him. "He is in his office now, I believe."

"I shall remain behind and keep watch, though it will not be easy if they use a private room, as Hartly suggested."

"What did Hartly do when he left the dining room?"

"He stood looking at the lake as if he wanted to jump in and drown himself; then Ponsonby joined him and they walked back and forth for a long time. I could not overhear them, but they seemed mighty interested in whatever they were saying. I believe Ponsonby is in it with him."

"Very likely. No one could be as foolish as Ponsonby pretends he is. Thank God Hartly is a gambler. He will be out of mischief for a couple of hours."

Moira left and Jonathon took the jewels to Bullion's office. Ponsonby was just leaving.

"Very kind of you to let us use your personal parlor, Bullion. I shall tell the others. Oh, and you will bring us a bottle of your excellent brandy."

He left, and Bullion took the emeralds.

"The gentlemen must be playing for high stakes tonight," Jonathon said in a casual way.

"Someone will lose a monkey and someone will make a tidy sum," Bullion replied. "I do not understand what makes them do it, but they will gamble, so I try to make them comfortable. It is a vice you would be wise to avoid, Sir David."

"It is a shocking waste of time and money. I shall waste my evening studying Latin instead. Will you send one of the girls up with a pot of tea? It helps to keep me awake."

"Happy to oblige. Will her ladyship like a cup as well?"

"A good idea. Do not trouble yourself, Bullion. I shall speak to Sally on my way up."

By the time he had finished his talk with Sally, Jonathon had learned the location of the family parlor where the card game would take place. The window looked out on the backyard and estuary, and he could overhear what was said within if the window was open.

"You ought to open the window a crack, Sally," he said, looking around at the modest room. "The gentlemen will be smoking cigars. They will suffocate if they have no air."

"I'll do that," she said, and went to lift the window an inch. "I'll get some saucers as well, to hold their cigars. Nasty, smelly things. The room will reek of them for a week. Your tea should be ready by now. I'll take it up."

"I shall take it myself and save you the trip." He tipped her a tupenny, and she was well pleased with his generosity.

Moira's head was throbbing from her prolonged session with Stanby. His manner was becoming hatefully romantic. He had held her hand and told her she was "a charmer, by gad." Had he said the same words to her mama? How could Mama have tolerated the weasel? Of course, it was partly his age that disgusted Moira, and he had not been that much older than Mama. Mama had no notion of his character. When one saw Stanby for the first time as a stranger, he would not strike one as ugly. Mama must have been dreadfully lonesome, missing Papa. She had been born and bred in the country, and had little experience of the world. Stanby would have had a cosmopolitan allure for her. But still, those gooseberry eyes! She shivered and pulled her wrap more closely around her shoulders.

When she heard a tap at the door, she thought it must be Jonathon and answered with no premonition of disaster. Mr. Hartly stepped in uninvited and closed the door. There was some severity in his expression that frightened her.

"You cannot come in, Mr. Hartly. I am alone," she said, and reached to open the door.

He blocked it with his body. A civil sneer descended on his handsome face as he said, "You were more obliging the first evening we met, madam."

"Sir David was next door on that occasion. I must ask you to leave, sir."

"And I, regretfully, must decline," he replied, and strolled into the bedroom.

Anger at his high-handed tactics warred with fear in her breast. "If you have come to harass me about being in your room this morning, I explained—"

"Your explanation was as false as that green glass necklace you wore at dinner."

A gasp escaped her. "Don't be absurd," she said. "Everyone knows the Crieff emeralds are genuine."

"I have no reason to doubt it, but we are discussing *your* necklace, miss."

"How dare you speak to me in this manner! Leave. Go away at once, or I shall call for help."

"Your lover won't hear you. He is belowstairs. Do you really want him to hear what I have to say?"

"Say what you have to say and leave, Mr. Hartly. I am in no mood for this. I have had an extremely trying evening."

"Have you indeed? I had not thought a tête-à-tête with a suitor would prove so demanding. What was it that upset you? Fear that the major would discover you are not Lady Crieff?"

Her face, already pale, blanched to white. Her gray eyes darkened in fear. "You are being ridiculous," she said, but she said it in a breathless, frightened whisper.

"No, madam. You are out of your depth. I have it on the best authority that Lady Crieff—a redhead, by the by—is still in Scotland. The Crieff case has been settled amicably out of court. Such stunts as you are endeavoring to execute ought to be done hastily, before some suspicious soul begins to ask questions. You would have done better to try your game with me the evening you arrived, as you intended. What stopped you? Did you fear my pockets were not deep enough?"

He saw her blank stare of incomprehension. "You?"

"Do you deny you lured me to your chamber?"

"An unfortunate error. I mistook you for a gentleman."

"I was not so blind. I knew at a glance that you were no lady. Now, who the devil are you, and what is your game?"

"I am Lady Crieff," she said.

"And I am King Louis of France. Your name is of no consequence in any case. You have two options. Either you give an account of yourself, or I tell Stanby the Crieff jewels are paste. You will find his affections are not so marble constant as you think. Charming as you are, Stanby will demand more than a pretty face in his mistress."

Color flooded her pale cheeks as that insult hit home. "For your information, he wants to marry me. At least I think—What has it to do with you, in any case? You do not fool me, Mr. Hartly. You are a Revenueman. It is Lord Marchbank you are investigating, not Lady Crieff."

"So you did plunder my dustbin. You really ought to have crumpled the letter up again. I am disappointed in you."

"What do you want?" she demanded, in a failing voice.

"I want—I demand—that you cease this charade. I am an officer of the law. It is true my job here has to do with smuggling, but I cannot in good conscience allow an upright citizen to be fleeced."

"Upright! The man is an outright scoundrel! You may feel differently after he has taken whatever money you have from you with shaved cards this evening."

"I thank you for the warning, but two wrongs do not make a right. You will cease this charade. It will be best if you leave the inn, quietly, without leaving a message for Stanby."

"No! I have waited too long. This is my only chance. You must understand, Mr. Hartly." She looked at his implacable face and gave a resigned sigh. Hartly was an officer of the law, that same law that upheld Lionel March's right to steal Jonathon's estate and her dowry with impunity.

"I am not unaware that Major Stanby's character is flawed," he said vaguely. "There have been minor incidents at the card table. One must take into account that he has spent his life defending the interests of his country. I do not wish to embarrass you, but the law is the law, and it is clearly your intention to break it. Do you have anywhere to go?"

With the possibility of being charged with a criminal offense hanging over her head, she was loath to reveal her identity. "No, and very little money."

"What of the Marchbanks?"

"They did not invite us to stay with them when we wrote, hinting," she said, hoping to incite pity.

Hartly began pacing to and fro in the small room. He saw the headache powders on the bedside table. He saw her pale, troubled face and felt a troubling spasm of pity. Whoever she was, she could not possibly be as bad as Stanby. Let her stay, and have a go at him, after he and Rudolph had left. When he spoke again, his tone had softened to conciliation.

"Perhaps we can strike a bargain," he said.

Hartly expected to see gratitude and wondered at her angry frown.

"I will not give information against Lord Marchbank!" she declared angrily.

"I have no need of further evidence against him. He has become so complacent, the evidence is there, for anyone to see."

"What did you mean, then?"

"You may stay on here at the inn until you have made other arrangements. You may even continue your masquerade as Lady Crieff, but you must tell Stanby you have decided against selling the collection. Use that fertile imagination of yours. Say you have arranged to sell the collection elsewhere; say you have found a patron whose company does not give you the megrims, or say you have decided to keep the jewels. Such an accomplished liar as yourself will think of something."

Moira felt a sting at that charge of being an accomplished liar, but her mind was too busy to harp on it. She saw no point in remaining at the inn if she could not execute her scheme of getting her money back. She was about to say so when an idea occurred to her. She might yet arrange some deal with Stanby behind Hartly's back. Hartly would be busy chasing after the brandy and the Gentlemen. She had nothing to lose by remaining.

"Very well," she said. "I agree. Thank you, Mr. Hartly."

"I expect you to keep your word, madam. Things will not go well for you if you do not."

Moira saw his scowling face through a mist of unshed tears. It seemed unfair that he could come storming down from London, carrying the full authority of the law with him, to destroy her life and

Jonathon's, and she could not do a single thing about it but tug her forelock and say, "Yes, sir." Lionel March was a lying, cheating, womanizing villain, but the law would defend him. The law sent a special envoy to try to stop Lord Marchbank. What real harm was he doing? He was an unsung hero to the starving poor of the countryside, but the law cared nothing for that. He had to be stopped. The law had to be maintained, for the good of villains like March.

"I understand," she said.

Hartly knew he ought to be feeling triumphant. He had stopped this impostor dead in her tracks. Stanby's money would go back to its rightful owner. But what would become of the soi-distant Lady Crieff?

"What will you do after you leave here?" he asked.

"Perhaps I shall buy a pair of breeches and join the army. It seems a military background puts one above the law."

"And David? What of him?"

"You have got what you want, Mr. Hartly. Pray spare me the hypocrisy of pretending a concern you do not feel."

He bit back a sharp retort. "I can give you some money, if that is a problem."

"I am not sunk to charity. Good night."

She walked to the door and held it wide. Mr. Hartly strode out, wearing a face like a bear. He had only been trying to help her. Why did she look at him like that, as if he were vermin? Damn her eyes! Why did he feel guilty? It was her youth, and of course her beauty. She looked so terribly vulnerable, standing alone, with her shoulders sagging, as if she had lost her last friend. So different from the laughing, teasing girl who had come to the inn two days ago.

He was wasting his sympathy. Women like that could take care of themselves. She would rush her case of paste jewels and her stormy gray eyes off to some other corner of the country and start over again.

Chapter Sixteen

It was much later when Jonathon went abovestairs. Knowing Moira was not feeling well, he did not disturb her but went to his own room. Before lighting his lamp, he noticed a ribbon of light beneath the sitting-room door. He went in and saw her sitting with her chin in her hands, the very picture of despair.

Moira had had two hours to think over their situation and had concluded that they were defeated.

"It is all over, Jonathon," she announced in a voice of doom. "Hartly knows we are not the Crieffs, he knows the collection is paste. He knows everything, except our real names. I would not tell him that. He has demanded that I tell Stanby the jewels are not for sale. If I do not, he will tell him everything and have us arrested into the bargain. I had no option but to agree. I wonder if he would be less concerned for Stanby's welfare if he knew the whole. Do you think I should tell him, and throw us on his mercy?"

Her news knocked Jonathon's own discovery out of his head. "The devil, you say. How did he find out?"

"He had someone checking up on us. It seems Lady Crieff is a redhead. She is still in Scotland."

"I wonder what put into his head to check up? No one else suspected anything."

"The man is a ferret. He weasels about with his sharp nose until he discovers everything. He knows all about Marchbank's operation. He will put him out of business as well."

"There you are wrong," Jonathon said, dropping onto the sofa and smiling. "Hartly ain't a Revenueman at all."

"Of course he is. What else could he be?"

"As big a rogue as Lionel March," Jonathon said, with a triumphant grin.

Moira's sagging shoulder straightened. A gleam of joy entered her eyes. "What have you learned? Tell me everything."

"I got Sal to open the window in the room belowstairs where they were to play cards, but they did not play. They were just talking. I hunkered down below the window and listened. I could not make out every word, but I heard enough. It made no sense for the longest time. They were talking about gross annual revenue and shares of the operation and such things, like a bunch of businessmen. But the business they were discussing was Cousin John's smuggling operation. You would not believe the fortune he is making!"

"A Revenueman would be interested in how the operation is run. He hopes to round up the whole gang."

"But why would he be discussing it with Stanby?

No, wait. There is more. The upshot of it is that Hartly said he had spoken to the Black Ghost, and the Black Ghost had agreed to sell the whole smuggling operation because his pockets were already full to overflowing, and he wanted to go off to London and spend his blunt. Now, you know that is a bag of moonshine. Peter don't actually run the ring at all. It is Cousin John who is in charge, and he has no notion of selling. He said Peter would take over when he is ready to hang up his hat.

"The story Hartly told is that he learned when he visited Cove House with us that the venture is for sale for fifty thousand pounds. Hartly is putting up fifteen, Ponsonby is putting up ten, and they are trying to talk Stanby into putting up twenty-five. It is nothing else but a swindle. Hartly will take their money and run. He is the one promoting it."

Moira sat stunned, unable to believe it. "It is some trick to catch Lord Marchbank," she said.

"Devil a bit of it. I tell you Hartly says the operation is for sale. He even showed Ponsonby and March some sheets of figures that he must have made up out of whole cloth, for the Marchbanks don't keep books. He told me this afternoon he never puts anything in writing. Bullion is in on it as well. He backed up Hartly's story. Hartly has some fellow claiming to be the Black Ghost who is going to take them on a tour of the whole operation tonight. That will be his groom, concealed under a black mask, I daresay. They are going to examine the ships, to see how the brandy is hidden below a false floor. Hartly is going to show them where the brandy is hidden when it is brought ashore. He says five thousand of the blunt will go as a bribe to Marchbank for his continuing cooperation, as he is the magistrate. And a couple of hundred for the Potter brothers, the simpletons who are the local Preventive men. He made it sound entirely plausible, I must say, and safe as money in Consols, only more profitable. I believe Stanby will go along with it. He says he has to check with his man of business to see if he has that much capital available, but his lips were watering at the prospect of an easy fortune."

"I don't doubt it. But do you mean to say Hartly is not with the Revenue Department at all? He is just a common thief?"

"I would take an affey-davey on it."

A tide of emotions surged over Moira as Jonathon convinced her this incredible story was true. Anger, a lust for revenge, and even a reluctant admiration were soon eclipsed by indignation. "And he had the audacity to call me a lightskirt!"

"Did he, by Jove?" Jonathon exclaimed, in high dudgeon. "I shall call him out."

"You will do nothing of the sort." A wicked smile gleamed in her eyes. "You must let me have the pleasure of dealing with Mr. Hartly. How I shall enjoy it!"

Jonathon sat, staring into the cold grate. "You ain't using your noggin, Moira. We ain't home free yet by a long chalk. Hartly still knows we ain't the Crieffs. He knows the jewels are fakes. If he tells March . . ."

"If he tells March about us, then we return the favor. *Point non plus.* He will have to come to some agreement with us. He does not hold all the tricks in his hand, as I thought. I shall enjoy meeting him again."

"It is a dangerous game you are playing, Moira,"

Jonathon said uncertainly. "I mean to say, there is so much money at stake that Hartly may just decide to—to do away with you. Be sure you have your interview in a safe place."

Moira felt no fear for her life. She did not think Hartly was a murderer, but she would heed Jonathon's advice and speak to him in a public place, just a little apart from other people. The settee in the Great Room would be perfect.

Sleep was impossible for Moira, with so many exciting matters on her mind. It was on the coming interview that she dwelt as she lay in bed, listening to the silence of the inn. Mr. Hartly would not be holding all the cards this time. He would not call her a lightskirt or threaten to have the law down on her head. It would almost be worth not recovering her money, to see him knocked off his high horse.

She figured out that the only reason he did not want her to sell March the paste jewels was that he wanted to steal the man's money himself. He was afraid March did not have enough for them both to rob him. But he could not force her to reveal that she was not Lady Crieff. That was the main thing. The choice of whether March would use his blunt to buy her fake stones or buy into Hartly's fake business was up to March. She would have to be very charming to the old lecher tomorrow.

It was an unhappy thought to fall asleep on. It would be much more interesting to be charming to Mr. Hartly. She regretted that he had such a low opinion of her, then berated herself as a ninnyhammer. What did she care for his opinion? He was a common swindler.

She finally slept, then awoke in the morning to see

jagged streaks of light dancing on the ceiling, where the ill-fitting curtains let the sun's rays in. She rose with a churning excitement in her breast, anticipating the interview with Hartly. He was usually at the table when she went down to breakfast. It was just a quarter to eight. If she hurried, she might see him alone, before March came down.

She rose and made a hasty toilette. The sun promised a warm day. She chose a blue mulled muslin gown and hastily ran a brush through her tousled curls. Examining herself in the mirror, she realized she did not look nearly as stylish as Lady Crieff. In fact, she looked much the way she looked at home—like any other provincial lady. No matter. She would spruce herself up before meeting the major. She could not take time to arrange a proper coiffure now.

She closed her door quietly when she left the room, to avoid disturbing other sleeping guests. The fewer people in the Great Room, the better. It was still a safe place. With the servants about, Hartly would not attempt any physical attack there, much as he would like to.

Chapter Seventeen

From the doorway of the Great Room, Moira saw Mr. Hartly sitting alone. He was just about to begin his breakfast. The room was deserted except for him and one elderly gentleman in the corner, reading a journal. Despite the strength of her position, she felt a sudden sense of trepidation as she approached Hartly's table. He looked so unassailable, so strong. If only he were not a scoundrel, he might have helped her. Two spots of red flared high on her cheeks, her eyes glowed with excitement, and her heart pounded mercilessly. Hartly looked up as she entered.

She walked straight to his table, smiled, and said, "Good morning, Mr. Hartly. It seems you and I are early birds. May I join you?"

He did not even bother to rise or say, "Good morning" but just nodded his grudging consent, with a contemptuous look that firmed her resolve. It stung like a nettle that he treated her as if she were of no account.

Hartly felt sure he understood her stunt at a glance. She had decked herself out as an innocent young provincial to work on his pity. And done her job well, too. She looked enchanting with her raven curls tumbling wantonly about her cheeks. That simple muslin gown was more fetching than all her silks and satins. She even wore an expression to suit her costume: a wide-eyed look of fear, tinged with determination. He prepared his ears for a tale of woe. What would it be? Two helpless orphans escaping a cruel stepmama? A wicked guardian who was forcing a match on her?

"I trust you have come to your senses, miss," he said in a hard voice. He would not offer her breakfast or even coffee. That would lend a friendly air to the proceedings. It was safer to stick to business with this engaging trollop.

"I have considered the matter," she replied.

"And?"

She gave him a bold look, all innocence vanished. "And decided you do not have a leg to stand on, Mr. Hartly."

His head jerked up. He directed a cool stare on her. "Indeed. I knew you were not wise, but until now I did not take you for a fool."

"Perhaps not, but you obviously mistook me for a greenhead. You, too, have been too slow about completing your business, Mr. Hartly. My investigations have disclosed that you are not who you say but a scoundrel trying to sell what does not belong to you."

He cocked a bold smile at her. "A case of the pot calling the kettle black, surely."

"If you wish. There all similarity ends, however. Your stunt is considerably more dangerous, sir. The

Black Ghost would have you drawn and quartered if I told him what you are about."

"He would not be such a fool as to harm a Revenueman."

"True, if you were a Revenueman, you would have some assurance of living beyond this day. A man who impersonates an officer of the law in order to execute a crime, however, is quite a different matter. He is in danger from not only the law, but also from the Gentlemen. I know what you are doing here, sir. You are trying to gull Stanby and Ponsonby into buying a share in the smuggling operation. I have not informed the Black Ghost of it—yet."

"You are mad as a hatter."

"I think not. Fifty thousand pounds is the price, of which you hope to get half from Stanby. That is why you do not want him to buy my jewels."

"Your collection of paste stones," he corrected.

Hartly swiftly conned his options. As she could quote the actual sum asked, he knew she was not bluffing. How could she possibly have found out? E'er long, he had his answer. Marchbank was certainly involved in the smuggling. He would have told her the operation was not for sale, but how did she know he was trying to sell shares in it? Stanby, of course! She had weaseled it out of him with smiles and kisses and God only knew what else. And now she sat before him, the picture of innocent virtue, in her girlish muslin gown. The knowledge of how she had got the information inflamed him to fury. When he spoke, he spoke in a voice so calm, it actually sounded bored.

"Stanby told you. I did not realize you were sharing his bed. It would have been wiser to wait until he had anted up the blunt. Gentlemen do not value what is given too freely—but that is your affair."

Moira bit down a howl of protest. How dare he? He had really gone too far this time. She took a deep breath to steady her voice before responding. "So it is. Let us get down to business, then. I know who you are, and you know who I am."

"You are not quite accurate, miss. I have no idea who you are, but I know who you are not—namely, Lady Crieff."

"And I know who you are not—namely, a Revenueman. If you breathe one word to Stanby, I shall inform not only him and Ponsonby, but also the Black Ghost, what you are up to. You will not make a penny. In fact, you would be extremely lucky to get out of Blaxstead alive."

Hartly was accustomed to danger from the Peninsula. He hastily considered his rather limited options with a cool head. Then he smiled and said, "May I pour you a cup of coffee, Lady Crieff? Remiss of me not to have done so sooner."

"Yes, you may; and yes, it was remiss of you." He poured the coffee. She took a sip and said, "Well, Mr. Hartly, what have you to say?"

"Damned fine coffee. Would you care for some gammon and eggs? Some toast, perhaps."

"No, I am rather particular as to whom I share food with."

"Unlike your bed!" The cynical words were out before he could stop them. He should be conciliating the chit, sweet-talking her into some sort of compromise, but all he could think of was her in Stanby's arms, that old man's hands caressing her, and he could not control his wrath.

Her eyes sparked dangerously. "Let us speak of

what concerns us, not irrelevancies. The major's pockets are not bottomless. I want his money; you want it."

"And may the better man win. I am speaking generically, including the female of the species."

"What do you mean, exactly?"

"I mean I will not interfere with your plans if you do not interfere with mine. What do you gain by handing me over to the Black Ghost, other than revenge? I, likewise, have nothing to gain by informing Stanby you are not Lady Crieff and your jewels are not worth a Birmingham farthing. We both proceed as if the other did not exist, and may the better man win. Come now, madam. You have the distinct advantage of me. If a pretty lady cannot use her charms to sway an aging bachelor . . ." He studied her a moment, chewing back a smile to see he had roused her ire. Her eyes were shooting daggers.

"Mind you," he said, allowing a disparaging smile to curve his lips, "I think you have gone a tad overboard on the dairymaid look this morning. Personally I find that touch of disarray charming, but I feel the major favors more sophistication in his ladies. On the other hand, you are on more intimate terms with him than I, so perhaps—"

"If you say one more time that I shared his bed, Mr. Hartly, I shall walk out that door and call the constable this instant!"

"You are being rash, my pet. Impersonating an heiress for the purpose of conning an innocent gentleman into buying glass beads is a hanging matter. There is hard evidence close at hand. I, on the other hand, have dealt only in words. Words are more difficult to haul into a court of law."

"You are a weasel! I knew the first time I saw you, asking Bullion for Major Stanby, that you were up to no good. I wondered what you had to do with Stanby. I thought you were his cohort. Now I see you had just chosen him for your victim."

"We have that in common, *n'est-ce pas*?"

"We have absolutely nothing in common, sir. And if you breathe one word to Stanby, you will have the Black Ghost to deal with. Good day."

She rose in a huff. Hartly rose and put his hand on her arm to stop her. "Do we have a bargain, Lady Crieff?"

Her nostrils flared in frustration. "Yes, we have a bargain. I would bargain with the devil himself if I had to. But I tell you in advance, you will not win. I plan to get my money, if I have to—to marry the scoundrel."

Hartly allowed his eyebrows to lift slightly. "I assumed that had already been settled between you and your lover. A lady who has compromised herself so grossly ought to have had a promise of marriage at least. It would be redundant of me to remind you of the evanescence of verbal bargains. We have already discussed that. Your best bet would be to scramble off to a bishop for a special license and haul Stanby in front of a vicar posthaste. I should be happy to stand as best man."

"I am sure we could find a better man than you, should the need arise. It would not be difficult. We would have only to look under the closest rock. Good day, Mr. Hartly."

She flounced out of the room, with his insults whirling in her brain: calling that old scarecrow, Stanby, her lover, saying she had compromised herself grossly, that she had spent the night with him.

She thought of a dozen cutting things she should have said. But she had achieved her aim. She had struck a bargain that neither would tattle on the other. Now it was up to her to see that Stanby chose her investment over Hartly's.

Hartly sat on alone, his gammon and eggs cooling on his plate as he reviewed his situation. The lady—woman—held a stronger hand than she knew. If she reported him to Marchbank, he would be whisked out of the inn and into irons before he had time to warn Stanby what she was about. She did not realize it, but Marchbank certainly would. He would have to move quickly. Settle the purchase of the smuggling operation before nightfall and hope she did not run to Marchbank in the meanwhile.

Within ten minutes, Ponsonby strolled into the room, fanning himself with a letter. He joined Hartly.

"Good day, Hartly. The major not up yet?" he asked.

"No, but Lady Crieff has paid me a visit. A new problem has arisen. Stanby has told her the whole story. She knows, from Marchbank, I daresay, that the smuggling operation is not for sale."

Ponsonby considered this a moment, then said, "She will cooperate. Stands to reason."

"What the devil are you talking about? She wants his money herself. And stands a better chance than we of getting it. She will resort to marriage if necessary."

Ponsonby frowned. "That would not be legal, would it? Marrying your steppapa." Hartly looked at him, bewildered.

"Ah, I have not told you the news," Ponsonby

said, holding up his letter. "I dashed off a line to Aunt Hermione the day after I arrived and had my man ride it off to London. Hermione knows everyone. I was curious about Lady Crieff's connection to the Marchbanks. I have the answer here. Moira and Jonathon Trevithick. That is who the Crieffs are."

"Who the devil are the Trevithicks?"

"A genteel family from Surrey. Old Stanby married their mama four years ago, when the youngsters were—well, younger youngsters. The mama died within a couple of months. Stanby took off with Moira's dot. Ten thousand, plus fifteen thousand he had wangled out of the estate by a mortgage. Took 'em for twenty-five thousand all told. The youngsters have had a rough go of it since then. Lady Marchbank is their cousin. She must be giving them a hand to diddle Stanby. That explains it all, eh? They are here to try their hand at getting their blunt back, same as us."

"Good Lord! What have I done?" Hartly whispered. "You haven't told Stanby?"

"No, but I . . . spoke rather harshly to Miss Trevithick."

"Ah, well, she'll understand. She is in the same boat with the rest of us. Dashed fine gel. Not a Bath miss. A regular man—er, woman, of bottom. Fooled me, with her coquettish ways. I always liked a dasher. Might offer for her when this is all over. She would not have me in the normal way, but if she don't get her blunt back, she might welcome a decent offer."

"I must speak to her, apologize." Hartly was just about to rise when Moira appeared at the doorway.

She had changed into a more stylish gown and

coiffure that did not become her nearly so well. Unfortunately, she was accompanied by the major. The major joined her and Jonathon at their table. She nodded at Hartly and said, "Good morning," as if this were the first time she had seen him that day. Her greeting to Mr. Ponsonby was noticeably warmer.

"Think she rather likes me," Ponsonby said aside to Hartly. "Mind you, she's a tartar about my drinking. She would cure me of my favorite vice. Well, perhaps my second favorite."

Hartly was not listening. He sat like a rabbit mesmerized by a snake as Moira flirted her head off with the major. Every smile and glance was a blow to his heart. Not because he was jealous, but because he knew how painful this charade must be for her. And he had added to her difficulties. He should have known she was an innocent. The first evening he had insulted her, he had sensed her maidenly innocence. Since then, he had heaped insult on injury, accusing her of all manner of indecency. She would never forgive him, and who should blame her? He would never forgive himself.

He rose and approached their table.

"I should like a word with you when you are finished with your breakfast, Major. Something has come up."

"I shan't be long," the major replied. "Let us meet in my room in half an hour."

"Very well."

Hartly tried to convey to Moira some of his chagrin, but as he was unable to use words, she misinterpreted his speaking glances as a challenge. She just lifted her pretty little nose and looked away. Hartly bowed and left.

Chapter Eighteen

"I say, you ain't having second thoughts about helping us?" Mott asked Hartly.

The three gentlemen met in Hartly's room after breakfast to discuss the latest development.

"We have no right to diddle Miss Trevithick out of her chance to recoup her losses," Hartly pointed out.

"Robbie's losses are as great," Mott objected. "Stanby took him for fifteen thousand—and my brother a mere schoolboy at the time."

"Dash it, Stanby took my papa for ten thousand," Ponsonby added, in an injured tone. "It was pure blind luck that he never saw me, for he ran tame at Papa's house for three months."

"But she is a lady!" was Hartly's only defense. He could not like to state baldly that he loved Moira Trevithick. "And Jonathon is only a lad."

"The pair of 'em are as good as an army. They are up to anything," Mott said.

Hartly replied, "You are forgetting she can squelch our whole deal by telling what she knows."

"And we can squelch hers," Ponsonby declared. "Dash it, Hartly, you said you have struck a bargain with her. Let it rest at that. We all have an even chance. Daresay Stanby will opt for her in the end. I mean to say—dashed pretty gel. She has the advantage when all is said and done."

"Who is to say Stanby is not deep enough in the pockets to snap up both bargains?" Mott suggested. "He has robbed dozens of people."

"He took in half a dozen others along with Papa with his shares in that gold mine," Ponsonby said supportively. "He must have hundreds of thousands on deposit. We ought to all get together—us and Miss Trevithick, I mean."

"Share and share alike," Mott said, warming to the idea.

"If need be, I would settle for half," Ponsonby said. "Better than nothing. We will each work on our own scheme. Whichever of us reels him in shares fifty-fifty with the other. That way, Miss Trevithick will not go home empty-handed, nor shall we. Put it to her, Hartly. She will listen to you."

"I am the last one she would listen to. It would come better from you, Ponsonby."

"She would think it was the drink talking. You do it."

"Both of you do it together," Mott said.

They agreed to call on her after Hartly's visit to Standby.

Hartly glanced at his watch. "I was to meet with Stanby in his room in half an hour. It is time I leave. We shall broach our idea to Miss Trevithick later."

"Be sure you let Stanby know we must have his answer by noon," Ponsonby mentioned.

"And his blunt by nightfall," Mott added, rubbing his hands in anticipation.

"We ought to warn Miss Trevithick we plan to move tonight," Hartly said. He was greeted with derision, but he stuck to his guns. "We have a bargain. I would do no less for a gentleman. I shall not take advantage of her being a lady, and so young."

Hartly left. As he entered the hallway, Moira was just coming up the stairs. He decided to speak to her at once, while he had the opportunity. She brushed past him with her nose in the air. Hartly took hold of her wrist and drew her to a stop.

"I have something important to say to you, Miss Trevithick," he said.

Miss Trevithick! The words sounded like thunder on the silent air. She wrenched her arm free and turned on him in fury. "So you know that, too. Congratulations, Mr. Hartly. I daresay you have already told Major Stanby?"

"Of course not," he said angrily. "Why did you not tell me from the start? Why did you let me believe . . . Well, you know what I believed."

"I told you Stanby was a scoundrel! I could hardly say more to a man who was posing as an officer of the law. You threatened to have me put in prison."

"You have known since last night that I am not a Revenueman."

"I have known from the moment I laid eyes on you that you are a bounder. You are the last person in whom I would confide anything. I would not trust you with my hound, let alone my own welfare."

Hartly took these insults without a blink. "We were both quick to leap to wrong conclusions. It happens I am not Mr. Hartly, and I am not a swindler either. Like you, I am here to try to regain a stolen fortune from Stanby."

"I do not believe a word of it."

"It is true, nevertheless. We ought to have made our positions clear from the beginning. We could have reached some arrangement."

"We have already reached an arrangement. You promised you would not tell him I am not Lady Crieff; therefore, you can hardly tell him I am Moira Trevithick."

"I had no intention of telling him! Dammit, I came here to suggest a truce. We might be of some help to each other. I am only thinking of your interest. If Stanby opts for buying into the smuggling ring, you may end up with nothing. We—Ponsonby and I—want to suggest a compromise. Whichever of us succeeds, we share even-Steven with the other. That way, no one goes home empty-handed."

She sniffed. "In other words, you know perfectly well I have the greater chance of success with Stanby, and you wish to cut yourself in. How very obliging of you, Mr. Hartly."

His temper broke at her continued intransigence when he was trying to help her. "You place a high value on your charms, madam. A man like Stanby will always put money before anything else, and the smuggling would make as much in a year as the Crieff jewels would make in a lifetime. It is your decision, however. I have done what I felt common decency required in making the offer."

Moira felt a twinge of doubt. What if Stanby opted for the smuggling investment? She and

Jonathon would be left high and dry. Half a fortune was better than none. Oh, but there was no trusting Hartly. He had some vile new scheme up his sleeve. Besides, his hateful arrogance made backtracking impossible.

She tossed her head imperiously. "Common decency demands that you leave off harassing me. We have our agreement."

Then she brushed past him and went to her room, where she reviewed their meeting, worrying whether she had made the wrong decision. She wondered, too, who he was if he was not Mr. Hartly. He had implied he was one of Stanby's victims. Could he be the man to whom Stanby had sold shares in that nonexistent gold mine in Canada? Hartly did not look like a man to be cheated at the card table. He was too wily for that. Who could he be?

Hartly continued on to the meeting with Stanby. It, at least, went well. Stanby had definitely decided to go snacks in the smuggling operation and was eager to get on with it.

"I have been thinking it is time I settle down," he said. "Lady Crieff has family in this area. She will like to live here. I shall build a mansion on the coast, where I can keep an eye on operations. As the major shareholder, the handling of the funds will be my responsibility. You and Ponsonby know what sums to expect. I am a gentleman. I shall not diddle you."

"No one is questioning your integrity, Major. If we cannot trust an officer, whom can we trust? Of course we shall drop in from time to time to visit. Er . . . you mentioned Lady Crieff. Am I to understand she has accepted an offer of marriage?"

The major gave a dismissing smile. "The ladies like to give a little show of reluctance. They think it indelicate to leap at the altar, but *entre nous*, I think she will have me."

This casual talk of building a mansion indicated that raising the wind would be no problem for Stanby. Hartly moved along at once to settle the finances.

"Ponsonby and I are arranging our funds this morning. The Black Ghost demands cash. He has another offer—from old Lord Marchbank, I believe. We must move quickly if we wish to secure this lucrative investment. Can you do it?"

"It happens I am meeting with my man of business this morning regarding another financial transaction I am involved in." Hartly mentally translated this to mean he was indeed buying the collection for cash. "I shall ask him to bring along the extra twenty-five thousand. I insist on being present when the cash is given to this fellow they call the Black Ghost. I mean no slur on your integrity, Hartly, but common sense dictates that in an investment of this sort, for cash, you know, with nothing in writing, every precaution must be taken."

"Why, truth to tell, Major, I welcome your company, and Ponsonby's as well. I would not care to meet the Black Ghost alone on some desolate beach at midnight. I plan to bring along a pistol. I suggest you do likewise, if possible."

"I never travel unarmed. There are too many rogues willing to rob a fellow's pocket. I don't know what England is coming to. We shall return to the inn when the deal is consummated and drink a toast to our success, eh, Hartly?"

"In our own unadulterated brandy," Hartly agreed.

"One 'gentleman' to another. Heh heh. There is more than one sort of gentleman nowadays, eh?"

"There certainly is," Hartly agreed with a bland smile that hid his rancor.

"I shall just get out my account books now and do my bookkeeping. I may want to transfer some investments as a result of this new venture. I like to keep a goodly sum in Consols, as they are not only safe as the Bank of England but liquid. I am withdrawing them for this current business. I shall sell my stocks in a certain shipbuilding company that is not performing so well since the war is over and put that into Consols. Being custodian of a large fortune is not all a bed of roses. It entails obligations."

"But a very pleasant obligation, is it not?" Hartly said, peering at the account book. The sums before him were dizzying.

"True." Stanby smiled. "Wealth is not a heavy burden to carry."

Hartly took his leave. The chore of acting left his temper frayed, but overall his mood was triumphant. It seemed Stanby did indeed mean to buy Lady Crieff's jewels. No doubt he had some scheme hatching to recover the money very soon after the wedding, but as Miss Trevithick had no intention of marrying him, that did not matter. She would just take the money and run. And he would never see her again. . . .

This was intolerable. He must see her, talk to her. Perhaps the lad could be of some help in a rapprochement. Bullion told him Jonathon had gone out for a ride. Hartly did not see Moira again until lunchtime, when she sat at Major Stanby's table, smiling and simpering and casting sheep's eyes at the old goat. Immediately after luncheon, she called her carriage and drove off to Cove House, where she remained until dinner.

The inn was busy that afternoon with callers from London, arriving with cases full of cash, arranging private meetings with Stanby, Ponsonby, and Hartly. Each gentleman was assembling his investment money.

During a quiet interval, Hartly had a word with Bullion. "Has the major asked to see the Crieff collection?" he said.

"That he did. I told him he would have to have Lady Crieff's permission. That shut him up. He does not want her to know he is so suspicious."

"Stave him off. Even if he comes with a letter from her, find some excuse."

Hartly did not tell Bullion the jewels were fakes, but he knew Stanby would realize it if he examined them by daylight.

"That I will, sir. Is your man all set for the meeting at midnight?"

"Gibbs is ready and waiting. You have the special brandy prepared for the celebration?"

"That I have." He touched his nose and nodded sagely. "It will be a dandy party."

"Until tonight, then."

Chapter Nineteen

Hartly wished to warn Moira that his plan was fast reaching its climax and she must move swiftly if she hoped to recoup her losses. She seemed determined not to allow him a moment alone with her. She stuck like glue to Stanby during dinner and afterward removed to the settee, still with Stanby. In desperation, Hartly followed Jonathon out to the estuary and had a word with him.

"Your sister told you what I am doing here?" he asked.

"No, I am the one who told her," Jonathon replied boldly. "I listened last night outside the window."

"You are a sharp lad. She is fortunate to have you to look after her."

Jonathon's chest swelled. "I just wish I could help share the burden of Stanby's company, but I am no good to her there."

"It is important that I speak to your sister. Do you think you could lure her upstairs to her room for a few moments?"

Jonathon frowned. "Why do you want to see her?"

"Something has come up. It is urgent. You may hold the reins of my curricle if you help me. I promise you I mean her no harm. Quite the contrary."

"I could be sick," Jonathon suggested, "but then I would have to stay abovestairs all evening."

"How about a cut finger? It would require a plaster, but not a whole evening in your room."

"I say, that is a jolly good idea." He drew out a clasp knife and pulled open the blade.

Hartly took it and replaced the blade before handing it back. "That will not be necessary, Jonathon."

Jonathon looked all around. "You had best call me Sir David here."

"Just so. I suggest you tie a handkerchief around your hand and tell your sister you cut yourself while picking up a piece of glass."

"I ought to smear something red on it, don't you think? I have it! I keep red ink in my room, for underlining my Latin book. I shall say I cut my finger while sharpening my quill. I shan't be a jiffy."

"I shall wait here a moment. We do not want to be seen entering together. Stanby might be suspicious."

"But why do you want to talk to Moira?"

"It is strictly business, Sir David."

"Oh, I was hoping p'raps you liked her," Jonathon said with the awful candor of youth. "She is really a very nice girl, you know. Not at all like Lady Crieff. She is afraid you have entirely the wrong opinion of her, from seeing her here, with her nice hair all twisted up in corkscrews, and wearing those trollopish gowns. Moira says that, other than having to make up to old Stanby, of course, having to look such a quiz in front of everyone is the worst part of this charade."

Hartly was interested to hear Moira had spoken of him. "You may assure your sister I have the highest regard for her, despite the corkscrew curls and décolleté gowns."

"She is very pretty, don't you think? All the fellows at home are running mad for her."

"Is there any special one . . . ?"

Jonathon shook his head. "No, she pays them no heed. Ever since Lionel March—that is what Stanby was calling himself when he married Mama—ever since he rifled our money, she has been obsessed with bringing him to justice. It is not just the money, though we are pretty hard-up without it. It is the principle of the thing, you see. She feels she owes it to Papa, and to Mama. Moira is strong on principles. She tells me March diddled you as well, Mr. Hartly. How did he cheat you?"

"He did not. It was my cousin, Robbie Sinclair, that he cheated at a rigged card game. Robbie was only eighteen. Robbie is Mott's younger brother."

"You mean Mott is not your valet?"

"He is my cousin, Lord Rudolph Sinclair. We were in the Peninsula together."

"By Jove!" Jonathon exclaimed, eyes open wide as a barn door. "Did you kill anyone?"

"More men than I like to remember, and Mott the same. He is a crack shot."

"Who would have thought it! About Mott, I mean. How, exactly, does your swindle work, Mr. Hartly?"

Hartly briefly outlined his scheme. Jonathon said, "So that is why you were in the tunnel the night you struck Moira with that club."

"Just doing a reconnaissance mission. I had no

idea it was you and your sister, or I would not have struck out. I had to know something about your cousin's operation to convince Stanby the deal was legitimate. I have regretted it, that it was your sister I struck."

"How did you know Marchbank is the chief?"

Hartly had not known Marchbank was actually the chief until that moment. "I realized he must be high up in the organization, as none of the Gentlemen are ever convicted. Surely he is not the Black Ghost?"

"No, that is Cousin Peter, from Romney. He is just used to frighten the Potters. You ought to have spoken to Cousin Marchbank. He would have been happy to help diddle Stanby, for what the bounder did to me and Moira."

"Yes, I regret not knowing from the beginning how matters really stood, but it is too late now. You go on in. I shall wait for five minutes, then go to your room to meet your sister."

Jonathon was enjoying himself so much, he was not eager to leave. "It is something like being at war, ain't it, Mr. Hartly? What was your rank? Were you a colonel?"

"Only a major, I am afraid. The title has acquired unhappy connotations since I met Stanby."

"What is your real name? Moira said you told her you ain't really Mr. Hartly."

"My name is Daniel. You had best run along now and 'cut' your finger."

"I shall make it my right hand. In that way, I shan't be able to write out my Latin verbs."

He bounced happily into the inn. Hartly stood, looking after him. He seemed a nice lad. He was happy Moira had had someone to bear her company during her hard years.

After five minutes, he went into the inn. Jonathon was just running downstairs, wearing a handkerchief soaked in red ink around his hand. It looked so horrible that Hartly was afraid Moira might faint. He followed Jonathon into the Great Room. Moira turned pale when she saw the ink-soaked cloth.

"Jonathon!" she gasped, jumping up from the settee.

Hearing her use her brother's real name, Hartly spoke up loudly to cover it. "Good Lord, what has happened?" he asked, rushing forward. A quick glance to Stanby told him he had not noticed Moira's slip.

"I was sharpening my quill when my knife slipped," Jonathon said. He wore an agonizing frown. "Could you come up and help me put a plaster on it, Lady Crieff?"

"I shall come at once," she said, and led Jonathon upstairs.

Hartly remained below a moment to share in the general consternation. When the talk turned to politics, he went quietly upstairs.

Jonathon had the sitting-room door open and beckoned him forward. "It worked pretty well, eh?"

Moira looked frazzled from worry. "You did not have to use the entire bottle of ink," she scolded. "I had best use a big plaster to lend credibility to this charade."

She got out her bandages and proceeded to cut off a large strip. "I want to thank you for leaping in to save me belowstairs, Mr. Hartly. I got such a fright when I saw all the red ink that I forgot myself. Do you think Stanby noticed?"

"I am sure he did not."

"You should have warned me what you were about, Jon." She continued patting the plaster in place. "I might have ruined the whole thing. What did you wish to discuss, Mr. Hartly?"

With a sly look, Jonathon went into his own room and closed the door behind him.

Hartly said, "My scheme is going forth tonight. Stanby has got his share of the money with him. I believe he also has the money to buy the Crieff collection. I suggest you rush your scheme forward as well. He will be in no mood to take any more chances by morning. At the very least, he will insist on having the jewelry assessed by a competent jeweler before turning over such a large sum."

"How can I rush it forward?" she asked. "It will look odd if I try to strong-arm him. He speaks of buying the jewels tomorrow morning and continuing on to London in the afternoon."

"With you?"

"Yes, that is what he thinks," she said, blushing. "I intend to flee out the window the minute I get my hands on the money."

"That is a harebrained scheme. He would not be ten minutes behind you. As soon as he got a good look at the collection, he would know your game."

"I only have to get to Cove House. Cousin Vera will say she has not seen me. Cousin John will hide the carriage and team at a neighbor's house until Stanby leaves the area. We have it all arranged. You are spoiling everything—all my years of saving and work." Her voice was edged with despair. It was mirrored in her stormy eyes. “Can you not hold off until tomorrow night, Mr. Hartly?”

“I fear that is impossible,” he said reluctantly. “We have everything arranged for tonight. I am not alone in this, Moira. I have to consider my partners.”

A little thrill raced along her veins to hear him call her by her own name. “Perhaps I can talk him into giving me the money tonight,” she said doubtfully.

“No, that will only alert him to mischief. Let your plans rest as they are.”

“But I may lose out entirely. You said yourself he would be doubly suspicious after being duped once.”

“I shall handle it.”

“How?”

“Did he put the money in Bullion’s safe?”

“Yes.”

“Then I know how to get hold of it. Pack your trunk and be ready to flee when I come for you.”

“I must know what you plan to do, Mr. Hartly.”

A reckless grin flashed. “I plan to shear a sheep. A black sheep. And now you must return below and simper and smirk at your fiancé. But you need not let him hold your hand.”

“He is not my fiancé! I did not say I would marry him. I would as lief marry a rat.”

“Your maidenly modesty forbids a quick capitulation. I assure you the major considers you his own. And I, for one, wish him every success.”

On this strange speech, he lifted her hand to his lips and placed a warm kiss on her fingers.

“I assure you I have no intention of marrying Stanby!”

"You misunderstand me, Moira. I did not mean *that* major!"

He gave her a strange smile, then left. The door to Jonathon's room opened with a suspicious alacrity the moment he was gone, and Jonathon stepped into the sitting room.

"I could not help overhearing what Hartly said. It looks as if our troubles are over, Moira. I shall begin packing. Cheer up, old girl. This is the last time you must endure March's company."

Moira stared at him as if in a daze. Her fingers tingled where Mr. Hartly had placed his lips on them. Should she try to get the money from Stanby tonight? It seemed an impossible thing to suggest. What would she do with such a sum, except leave it in the safe, where it already sat? Stanby would be bound to suspect if she kept it in her room. Could she trust Mr. Hartly, who was not Mr. Hartly at all but a total stranger? Did she have any option?

"You had best stay up here, Jonathon. You have got red ink smeared on your other hand as well. It looks nothing like blood."

Moira returned belowstairs, but she was so nervous that she soon claimed a headache and went back upstairs, to continue her worrying there.

Chapter Twenty

At a quarter to twelve, Jonathon tapped at Moira's door and entered, to find her sitting on the edge of her bed with her trunk packed. She and Jonathon had discussed the matter fully. Having little choice, she had decided to go along with Mr. Hartly's suggestion.

"I am going to follow them when they leave the inn," Jonathon said. "They are meeting at the cove by Marchbank's place. I figure if there is any trouble with the Gentlemen, I can let Cousin John in on it, and he will help out."

"I have been thinking and thinking," Moira said distractedly. "I have written to Cousin Vera, telling her of the change of plans, for she expects us tomorrow. Take her my note, Jon, and warn Lord Marchbank what is afoot. It was reckless of Mr. Hartly to use Marchbank's cove."

"It lends an air of authenticity to the thing, though."

"I am so nervous. Do you think we can trust Mr. Hartly?"

"He is a right one," Jonathon said warmly. "With him and Mott at the helm, nothing will go wrong. They have seen stronger action than this in the Peninsula."

"What do you mean? You said nothing of the Peninsula. Was Mr. Hartly in the army?"

"Of course he was. He was a major. Did he not tell you?"

"No!" A major! "The major considers you his own." "I did not mean *that* major!" Was it possible . . . Her cheeks felt warm.

"And Mott an officer as well. A crack shot. Whoever would have thought that man milliner would know how to use a gun? Well, I am off. Where is the letter?"

Moira handed him the letter. She considered going with Jonathon but felt someone ought to remain at the inn with the money and the jewelry, in case Stanby had some sly plan to return before the others and run off with the lot.

Jonathon rode to Cove House. It was a nice, scary ride, with the dark water shimmering on one side of the road and black trees whispering their menace on the other. Cove House was in total darkness, but he knew the back door was always left on the latch in case of an emergency with the Gentlemen. He entered and crept up to Lady Marchbank's chamber. She was a light sleeper. Her husband's career involved so many strange doings that she was not at all surprised to see Jonathon appear at her bedside at close to midnight. With a blink of her eyes she was wide-awake. She snatched her spectacles from the bedside table, read the note through, and said, "Marchbank ought to know about this."

"Yes, I want to speak to him."

They went together, Lady Marchbank wrapped in a faded woolen housecoat, with a cap tied under her chin.

Marchbank listened to what Jonathon had to say and read Moira's letter. "So that is what is afoot," he said, nodding. "Moira ought to have told me."

"She did not want to lead Hartly to you. He could still report you, even if he ain't a Revenue inspector. Not that he would, but we did not know the whole until tonight."

"I have lost two nights' work for no reason," Marchbank said. "Speak to Jack Larkin, in the stable, Jonathon. He will see young Hartly is not disturbed. If any of the Gentlemen come at night, Jack deals with them. But they have been told to lie low until Hartly leaves. Not a Revenueman, eh? That is good news. I dislike to think London is taking an interest in me."

Jonathon went down to the stable, where he found Jack Larkin napping, fully dressed, mounted on a bay mare. Jonathon jostled him awake and gave him Marchbank's message. Larkin nodded and was soon asleep again. It was said of Larkin that he could sleep standing up and ride sound asleep.

By the time Jonathon reached the cove, the Black Ghost had already arrived. Jon was sorry he had missed the arrival. The cluster of men—Stanby, Ponsonby, Hartly, and his batman, posing as the Black Ghost in a black hat, mask, and domino, stood in a circle with their heads bent. They were limned in charcoal against the silver sky, with a dog-starred moon high above and the rippling ocean below. The sight gave the strange illusion of some medieval ritual. Jonathon could not hear their words, but he could hear the light clink of gold as the bags were handed to the Black Ghost, who shook hands with them all in turn before leaping astride a huge black stallion. The horse reared on its hind legs, whinnying. The Black Ghost emitted one eerie laugh, raised his arm in farewell, and disappeared into the black shadows of night, leaving only the ghostly echo of horse beats behind.

The remaining gentlemen began to climb up the embankment to recover their mounts. Jonathon turned back to the inn, to avoid being seen on the road in front of them. He was soon rushing into Moira's room.

"He did it! Hartly pulled it off. I wish you could have seen it, Moira. It was better than a stage play. They are on their way back here now. It won't be long. Are you all set to leave?"

"We cannot leave yet. Hartly has got his own money, and Ponsonby's. He has not got mine. Stanby was putting up only twenty-five thousand. My money is still in Bullion's vault."

Jonathon, caught up in the thrill of the moonlight escapade, had not thought of this.

"I begin to think it was all a ruse to keep us from disturbing his plan, Jon," Moira said grimly. "All Mr. Hartly cared about was his own money. He will leave the inn as soon as Stanby retires, collect his ill-got gains from the man acting the Black Ghost, and never be seen again. We have been outwitted."

"You have had too much time to sit, fretting," Jon said. "You mistrust every man because Stanby is such a rotter. I shall run downstairs and see what is afoot. I can hide behind the sideboard in the passage outside the Great Room."

Jonathon could hear the merry laughter coming from the Great Room even before he reached the bottom of the stairs. Bullion was pouring brandy; the gentlemen were making toasts to their success and their new venture. He listened but could hear no clue to Hartly's plan to help Moira. Jonathon did not believe for a moment that Hartly meant to leave him and Moira out in the cold. He did not have to warn them he meant to move tonight. They would never have guessed it. Since he had told them, and warned them to have their trunks packed, then obviously he meant to look after them.

The sound of merriment rose higher. Ponsonby was singing now, a ribald song. His voice began to peter out. Jonathon peered into the room and saw that Ponsonby had passed out. Bullion was still filling the other gentlemen's glasses. They were all putting it away at a great rate. Major Stanby began to weave to and fro, then sat on a chair with a jerky motion that suggested he had fallen rather than sat voluntarily.

Within a minute, his head fell forward onto the table. Ponsonby rose from the floor like Lazarus rising from the dead.

"Is he out?" he asked Hartly.

Hartly put his finger to his lips to hush Ponsonby. He shook Stanby's shoulder and said in a heavy voice, "Come now, Major, a toast to His Majesty." The head on the table did not stir. The doctored brandy had done the job.

Ponsonby took hold of Stanby's hair and lifted his head, looked at his closed eyes, and let the head bounce unceremoniously onto the table. "Right, he's out. Let's go," he said.

Hartly grinned. He handed Bullion a jingling leather bag. "Bullion, you did well. If you would care to get the money out of the safe, I shall alert Lady Crieff we are ready to depart."

"I have something I want to put in the safe for Stanby," Ponsonby said, and darted from the room.

Jonathon ran quickly upstairs before he was seen. He did not tap on Moira's door but just stuck his head in and said, "You was dead wrong, Moira. Hartly is getting your blunt now. He will be here in a minute. Now, ain't you ashamed of yourself, not trusting him? I told you he was a right one." Then he ran to his own room to call a servant to take down the trunks.

Moira just stood, frozen to the spot. He was coming! He had told her the truth! Her ordeal was over. The two or three minutes until he came seemed an eternity. When the tap sounded at her door, she walked as one in a trance and opened it. Mr. Hartly came in and handed her a leather valise.

"The money is there. Twenty-five thousand," he said, opening the case to show her.

She just looked at it. "Oh," she said. After a moment she added, "Thank you, Mr. Hartly," in a very small voice.

"My pleasure, Miss Trevithick." They stood, gazing at each other in the silent room. "It was very good of you," she said stiffly. Her silvery eyes continued gazing uncertainly into his.

A slow smile began at his lips and spread over his face. "Do you know, I have a feeling Lady Crieff would have been more forthcoming in her thanks," he said, setting aside the valise and seizing her hand.

"You must think I am horrid," she said, blushing at the memory of past indiscretions.

"Yes indeed. It was unspeakably vile of you to wish to recover what was stolen from you, to say nothing of your cowardice in tackling one of the greatest villains who ever blotted the face of England. We shall not even mention your wretched ingenuity in impersonating Lady Crieff, and doing it well enough to fool us all."

She smiled uncertainly at these ambiguous compliments. "Where will you go now?" she asked.

"I had planned to return to Hanover Square when things are settled with Stanby."

"To Lord Daniel's house?"

"'Actually, to his father's house. Lord Daniel is only a younger son of Lord Tremaine. The elder son does not usually enter the army."

"Lord Daniel was in the army?" she asked, as realization dawned. He nodded. "Was he, by any chance, a major?"

"Just so."

"You?"

"Guilty as charged. Will you go to Cove House, or home to Surrey?"

"Do you think it would be safe to go home?"

"Bow Street will be here by morning to take Stanby into custody. He is wanted in connection with dozens of crimes, including bigamy. He never was legally married to your mama, Moira, so you need not fear he has any claim to your money. We would have called Bow Street in earlier, except that some of his crimes are difficult to prove. The fifteen thousand he got from my cousin Robbie Sinclair, for instance, at a rigged game of cards. That is what brought me down to Blaxstead. Ponsonby's family—his real name is Lord Everly, by the by—was fleeced by being sold shares in a nonexistent gold mine. The family gave up on recovering their blunt. Everly was told that if he could recover it, it was his. Stanby had never met him, so when he discovered that Stanby was here, he came after him, using a different name. He plans to leave the shares Stanby sold his papa in Bullion's safe, along with the Crieff jewels. We would not want the major to be left empty-handed."

Moira listened, waiting to hear what crime Stanby had perpetrated on Hartly. "And you? Had you no personal interest in catching Stanby? I mean—Mott and Ponsonby and I all recovered our money. What do you get for all your work?"

"I hope I get the girl?" he said questioningly, drawing her into his arms. Moira did not resist.

As his lips found hers, she had the strange sensation that, while her head was spinning, her heart had stopped beating altogether. The embrace began as a light, tentative touching of the lips but soon escalated to scalding passion. His lips firmed as his arms tightened inexorably around her in a vicelike grip, nearly suffocating her. A wave of golden exultation unlike anything she had experienced before washed through her. It felt as though a big golden sun were shining, warming her to her very core.

Hartly lifted his head and gazed at her with dark eyes. Then he lowered his head, and she felt a trail of fiery kisses over her eyes and ears. His palm brushed her fevered cheek and moved to cup her chin, tilting her head upward. She saw the tenderness of love glowing softly on her. "Do I get the girl?" he asked, in a ragged voice.

A smile trembled on her lips. "Yes, if you want me. I cannot imagine what you would want with such a depraved creature."

His matching smile stretched to a grin. "You are sadly lacking in imagination, milady. I want—this," he said, and kissed her again.

Wrapped up in their love, they did not hear the door open. "I say!" Jonathon exclaimed joyously. "Does this mean he has asked you to marry him?"

Moira drew away in embarrassment. "Certainly not!" she said. "I was just . . . just thanking Mr. Hartly . . . that is, Major—I mean Lord Daniel. Oh, what should I call you?" she asked in confusion.

"Call me 'my fiancé,' until we are married. That will solve the question." When she opened her lips to object, he raised a finger. "No welshing on a bargain. You said I got the girl!"

Jonathon rushed forward to pump Daniel's hand. "I shall call you Daniel. Are you coming home with us, or are we going to your place?"

"That will be up to my fiancée," Daniel replied. "Eventually, we shall remove to Oakdene, my place in Sussex, when you are a little older, Jon."

"Oh, do come home with us first," Jonathon said. "Moira is always saying we need a man around the place, and now that we have our blunt back, we can begin doing all the things that need doing. The roof needs releading, and there is that pasture Papa meant to tile, and—"

Daniel nodded. "As I have an excellent bailiff, perhaps it would be a good idea to go to your place first. But before those decisions are made, I would like to take Moira to Cove House. There will be a certain amount of unpleasantness here tomorrow. We can leave for the Elms in a few days. Moira, does that suit you?"

Moira did not care where she went, as long as she was with Daniel. "That will be fine," she answered in a daze.

"Excellent. I want to take a couple of barrels of your cousin's brandy back with me. I shall deliver you to Cove House now. Ring for someone to take down your trunks, Jon."

"I have already done it, but I do not want to go to Cove House with Moira. I should like to stay here," he said. "I have never seen a Bow Street Officer. I daresay he will be carrying a gun. You shan't forget to take me for a ride in your curricle, Daniel? You promised. You will let me take the ribbons when we get home, won't you? Moira, you have not forgotten you promised I could have a curricle if we got our blunt back from March."

"For goodness' sake, Jonathon," Moira exclaimed. "Stop chattering. You make my head ache."

"But you will let me stay here with Daniel?"

Daniel said, "If you are in the next room and very quiet, I daresay we shall forget you are there when Moira leaves."

Jon gave a cheeky grin. "Oh, you mean you want me to leave so you two can snuggle some more."

"Just so," Daniel replied blandly.

Jonathon left, and Daniel resumed his interrupted lovemaking.